ID

D1588243

Phemie needed normality, not ideas put in her head with regard to Gil Fitzwilliam. The man might indeed be sex on legs, but that was beside the point.

No matter how sexy any man was, no matter how he might make her feel, no matter how her thoughts and body went haywire when he was around, it would all be meaningless in the end. Long-term relationships weren't for her. Marriage wasn't for her. Having her own children was something she could never do.

Whilst she loved and adored her brother completely, she couldn't risk becoming pregnant and giving birth to a child with Down's Syndrome.

She'd lived that life. She'd watched her parents for years, seen their long-suffering patience almost running out on several occasions. The way they hadn't been able to pay the proper attention to her because of Anthony, the way they'd had to rely on her to take up the slack. Phemie felt as though she'd aged prematurely, especially throughout her teenage years. There had been no time for parties, no time for experimenting, no time for boyfriends. She'd been a surrogate mother to her sibling.

She loved her family, more than anything, and if she had to do it all over again she would. But she'd vowed never to put a child of her own through what she'd been through—and, as such, the only way to completely ensure that never happened was never to have children.

Caring for others was what she was good at, and that was what she was busy doing. Working in the Outback, caring for the community, helping others in any way she could. Those were the choices she'd made and she was determined to stick to them. The emotions Gil Fitzwilliam evoked deep within could mean nothing to her...

Lucy Clark is a husband-and-wife writing team. They enjoy taking holidays with their two children, during which they discuss and develop new ideas for their books using the fantastic Australian scenery. They use their daily walks to talk over characterisation and fine details of the wonderful stories they produce, and are avid movie buffs. They live on the edge of a popular wine district in South Australia, and enjoy spending family time together at weekends.

Recent titles by the same author:

A BABY TO CARE FOR
NEW BOSS, NEW-YEAR BRIDE
BRIDE ON THE CHILDREN'S WARD
SURGEON BOSS, BACHELOR DAD

A BABY FOR THE FLYING DOCTOR

BY
LUCY CLARK

First published in Great Britain 2010
Large Print edition 2010
Harlequin Mills & Boon Limited,
Eton House, 18-24 Paradise Road,
Richmond, Surrey TW9 1SR

LP

© Anne and Peter Clark 2010

ISBN: 978 0 263 21117 7

Harlequin Mills & Boon policy is to use papers that are
natural, renewable and recyclable products and made
from wood grown in sustainable forests. The logging and
manufacturing process conform to the legal environmental
regulations of the country of origin.

Printed and bound in Great Britain
by CPI Antony Rowe, Chippenham, Wiltshire

A BABY FOR THE
FLYING DOCTOR

To Vikki—
thanks for your generosity in sharing your
experience and knowledge about Down's.
It was greatly appreciated.

Eph 2:10

CHAPTER ONE

EUPHEMIA GRAINGER made her way along the corridor of the old refurbished train, measuring her steps in time with the sway of the carriage. It was quite exciting. She'd never been on a train before, well, not this sort. This was a long-distance train that cut its way from west to east across the wide brown land of Australia. She'd boarded the train at the Didja station, but there were still another two full days of train travel before she arrived in Sydney.

Phemie smiled, pleased she'd finally decided to do something for herself...well, sort of for herself. Anthony had been a big part of her decision to travel by train and she was definitely the sort of person who put others first.

Being raised with a disabled brother—a brother she loved dearly—had taught her that her needs generally came second. Sometimes, when she'd been growing up, she'd been jealous of the attention Anthony received but had known it was necessary. After she'd experienced those moments of envy, she would be swamped immediately by guilt. It was hardly Anthony's fault he'd been born with Down's syndrome.

She was excited to see him on Friday morning when he and his friends would join the train journey for the last day of adventure. Her smile widened as she thought about Anthony. It had been three weeks since she'd last seen her brother and the excitement started to bubble because she knew just how much he'd enjoy train trav—

'Excuse me,' a deep, rich English voice said from behind her, and Phemie immediately turned, looking up at whoever had spoken.

'Sorry.' She moved to the side of the small train aisle so he could pass and glanced up, craning her neck because of his height. 'I didn't realise I was blocking the corridor— Professor Fitzwilliam!'

The words were out of her mouth before she could stop them.

Gilbert Fitzwilliam was startled as he looked down at the petite blonde woman before him, her large blue eyes looking up into his own brown ones. How could she possibly know who he was…unless she was connected with the medical community in some way? It was the only answer and even though she looked about twenty years old, she could still be a conscientious medical student, nurse, dietician or perhaps an intern.

She put out her hand and he automatically took it. He'd been shaking hand after hand for the past eleven months. Soon, though, it would all be over. One more conference in Sydney and his travelling fellowship would technically be over. Once he returned to the UK and completed the paperwork, he'd be officially unemployed. What he would do next, he had no idea. At the moment, though, he needed to keep busy.

'I've read your papers.' The pretty blonde nodded enthusiastically. 'Amazing stuff.'

Stuff? She was still shaking his hand, her slim fingers warm and inviting. When she'd initially looked at him, she'd had the most engaging smile on her lips and he'd been instantly captivated by her, by this…stranger. This stranger who knew who he was and had found his scientific papers to be amazing 'stuff'. 'Uh…well…' He cleared his throat and raised an eyebrow before looking pointedly at their hands.

'Oh. Sorry.' She immediately let go. 'I guess I hadn't expected to find you here. On the train, I mean. Last place in the world. Going to Sydney on a train, across Australia. Who would have thought?' Good heavens. She was babbling. She never babbled. Well, not unless she was nervous. Was she nervous? If so, why was she nervous? What on earth did she have to be nervous about? The fact that the man before her was one of the world's leading experts on emergency medicine— her particular forte—couldn't possibly have anything to do with it!

'I'm pleased you found them so informative.' Gil looked into her upturned face, once again struck by her beauty. The afternoon light coming through the window beside them gave her an ethereal glow that made her blonde locks radiant, her blue eyes sparkling with a pleasure he'd never thought his medical writing could promote.

They stood staring at each other, captured in a strange bubble in the middle of an aisle in a train carriage. Phemie couldn't believe how distinguished and handsome Professor Fitzwilliam was in real life. She'd seen several stock photographs of him as she'd waded her way through medical journals and articles he'd written and even though she'd known she would be seeing him at the conference in Sydney, given he was the guest of honour, she hadn't expected to come this close to him. Not like this. Not in a personal rather than a professional capacity.

His brown hair was cut short even though she was certain that if he were to let it grow a little longer, it would have a definite curl to the ends. Flecks of grey peppered the sides but instead of making him look old, they gave him a distinguished air of authority.

It was his eyes, however, that had her staring, forgetting all her manners. The rich deep brown irises were flecked with golden swirls, making her feel both wild and yet safe at the same time. It was an interesting sensation and one she'd never experienced before, but it wasn't every day she stood gazing at a man she classified as medical royalty.

The train lurched, breaking the moment, bringing them both back to reality with a jolt. Phemie lost her balance, putting a hand to the wall to stop herself from falling but instead of finding hard wood panelling, she found hard muscular arms coming around her as Professor Fitzwilliam steadied her.

'Easy there.' He stood firm as the train continued to bounce around. The first thing that assailed his senses was her sweet yet subtle scent. He'd never known someone could smell like sunshine before but this young woman did. The second thing he noticed was the way his arm seemed to mould naturally to her shape. Her hand was resting on his shoulder, his hand at her waist.

As they wobbled back and forth, Phemie somehow managed to steady her feet, bending her knees slightly so she swayed better with the rhythm of the train. Now that she had herself back on track, she should really let go of him, although it appeared she was having trouble sending the signals from her brain to her limbs.

All she'd been able to concentrate on was the feel of his warm skin beneath his thin cotton shirt and how, due to her lack of height, her eyes rested at his chest level. Where his tie would ordinarily reside, there was now an open shirt, revealing a smattering of dark brown hair. She breathed in and tried not to crumple further into his arms as her senses were assailed with a light spicy cologne that she'd always loved.

He looked at her, momentarily surprised to find just how close they'd become. The train jolted again and he increased his grip. His gaze flicked from her lips to her eyes and back again and the urge to actually kiss this woman, this complete stranger, was utterly overwhelming.

How ridiculous. He didn't *do* instant attractions. He didn't *do* romance. He didn't *do* relationships. He'd been there, done that and his world had ended in despair. Work was the only thing that interested him. He could lose himself in work. He could write articles, develop new techniques. He could lecture and pass on information because work never let him down. It occupied his every waking moment and kept his mind busy. At least, that's the way things had been until a few minutes ago…before he'd had his arms around the beautiful blonde.

The train levelled out but it took Phemie a moment or two to process this fact. Her mind was too busy trying to decipher whether Professor Fitzwilliam had actually just looked as though he intended to kiss her! Or had that been her own imagination? She was already half in love with the man's mind. He was so brilliant, so insightful and now that she'd come face to face with him, so…incredibly gorgeous. She did her best not to sigh out loud.

'Uh…' Phemie licked her lips and edged backwards, almost flattening herself against the wall. 'Thanks.'

'For what?' He'd let her go. He was no longer

touching her and yet his body still tingled and buzzed from the powerful electric jolt he'd received when holding this delightful young woman in his arms. The fact that she was the first woman to have elicited such a response since his wife was something he didn't really want to think about.

'For…uh…' Oh, come on, Euphemia. Get that intelligent brain of yours working, she silently scolded herself. 'Stopping me from falling.'

He nodded once. 'Yes. Right. Good. Well you're…uh, welcome, Miss…' He fished for her name because deep down inside he simply *had* to know who she was.

'Grainger. Dr Euphemia Grainger.' She was about to shake his hand again but caught the impulse in time. No. No more touching of the muscular and well-toned English professor.

His eyebrow went up again in surprise at her name. Doctor, eh? So she was obviously older than he'd initially thought. It certainly helped explain how she'd known his identity.

'As I've already mentioned, I've read all of your papers.' Her smooth tones washed over him and he found her Australian twang rather delightful.

'I remember.' His lips twitched into a smile. 'Apparently they were amazing…stuff.'

She wrinkled her nose at the way he said the word, then a bright smile spread across her face, lighting her eyes. The overall effect made Gil suck in a breath. 'Sorry. That's my younger brother's influence rubbing off on me. He uses the word like water.'

Older sibling. Doctor. Stunning. Good taste in reading material. Gil filed away these points. 'So...Euphemia.' He rolled her name around on his tongue. 'That's a rather different name.'

'Family one, I'm afraid.'

'You don't like it?'

She shrugged. 'I guess you could say I'm used to it. I also like the aunt I was named after so I guess that helps.' Phemie glanced behind him and saw someone else was heading in their direction in the already overcrowded narrow, swaying corridor. She gestured to the person coming through and both she and Professor Fitzwilliam flattened themselves against the walls. She was highly conscious of where he was standing, trying to avoid being pushed into him, but the train lurched once more, causing her to press right up against the one man she was trying to avoid.

The heat was instant. The pressure, the awareness she had of him. It was starting to become too much for her. The person passing them stumbled as the train wobbled and Phemie held firmly onto the professor. She couldn't move until the other man had passed them by.

'Very squashy,' she whispered as her body pressed up against his. She didn't want to breathe in his scent. She didn't want to be aware of how incredible his body felt beneath her hands.

Gil worked hard at keeping his hands by his side, determined not to hold her again. Her chest was pressed against his body and the effort to ignore all sensations called on all his inner strength. Humour. Humour would be the only way to diffuse this situation. He grinned down at her. 'I don't know about squashy. I find this sort of situation helps you get to know complete strangers rather quickly.'

Euphemia was amazed at how a simple thing like a smile could transform someone's face. Small laughter lines appeared around his eyes and those rich brown irises made her think of melting chocolate. His mouth was curved, showing a tiny glimpse of white teeth, and she realised the whole awareness thing she was feeling with him was ridiculous and extremely temporary. Making light of the situation did seem the best option. She would follow his lead.

Returning his smile, the warmth of his body was still flowing against hers, all the way to her toes, but she did her best to ignore it. 'It most certainly does.' She looked down the aisle and was astonished and embarrassed to find the elderly man had passed them and was almost through the door at the other end of the carriage, leaving them both room to move.

Phemie shifted back immediately and straightened her light cotton jacket. Twice she'd been up against him, meaning she had twice the amount of wild awareness coursing through her body, yet somehow she had to ignore it. He was Professor Fitzwilliam, for goodness' sake. Her superior not only in qualifications but in experience. She looked at him, desperate to think of something to say that would make her sound intelligent and yet get her away from him as soon as possible.

'I'd best get back to my cabin.' She even pointed to where it was. Way to go, Phemie, she silently congratulated herself. No doubt the next Nobel Peace Prize candidate.

He nodded but when she didn't immediately move, he cleared his throat and put a bit of distance between them. It was strange. They were no longer near each other, she was about to leave, and Gil was struck with a burning desire to prolong their contact. He was intrigued by this young woman and he quickly decided that as long as he kept things businesslike, there was no reason why he couldn't chat with her. Perhaps he could assist her in a medical capacity? Help her to choose the area she might want to specialise in? Act as a sort of sounding board for any ideas she might have? After all, they still had a few days to go before arriving in Sydney and it would be foolish to completely ignore her...not after holding her so firmly in his arms.

'Look, Dr Grainger.' Yes. It was much better when he thought of her like that rather than as a desirable woman who had been in his arms twice in the past five minutes. 'I hope you won't think me too impertinent if I invite you to join me for a cup of tea in the lounge car. We could...discuss my papers or talk about the most recent break-throughs in medical science.' Business. He needed to keep everything on a professional level.

His smooth deep tones washed over her and his rounded English vowels made her knees quiver. 'Oh.' One-on-one time with Professor Fitzwilliam! Her first instinct was to immediately accept but she'd learned long ago to temper those first instincts because responsibility always came first. She was the older sibling, the carer, the reliable friend who put other people's needs before those of her own.

'Think it over,' Gil said when it seemed she was having difficulty replying. 'It's a long journey and we'll no doubt "bump" into each other again.' And for some reason, he secretly hoped it was literally as well as figuratively. With that, he turned and headed back the way he'd come, but before he could reach the door, she spoke.

'I'd love to sit and chat with you.'

He looked over his shoulder, pleased with her answer. 'Great.'

'Especially about your latest journal article or your research developments. However…' she shrugged apologetically '…it's just that…um…I need to get my head around my conference presentation.'

'You're going to the conference?' Gil's eyebrows hit his hairline. Not an intern, then. Fully qualified specialist? Dr Grainger's age kept increasing in his mind. His lips twitched at the thought. Poor woman. She was becoming older and older the more he discovered about her.

'It's my first time presenting,' she confided with a laugh that ended in a sigh. 'I'm rather nervous, though.' She spread her hands wide. 'I guess that must sound silly to someone like you who can get up and give brilliant keynote speeches with ease and clarity. Still, I'm looking forward to it.' She didn't want the man to think she was incompetent.

'Don't let the fact that I've done many speeches fool you. I still get a little nervous.'

'You do?'

'Of course.' He didn't want to talk about himself, he wanted to learn more about her. 'I must say, Euphemia, it's very impressive you've had a paper accepted.' He knew the quality of the presenters at the conference and realised Dr Grainger must indeed be an exceptional doctor if her paper had been chosen. 'And you're going all the way to Sydney by train?'

'Yes. More time to finalise things, at least that's what I keep telling myself. I just want everything to be perfect.'

'And that's your cabin?' He pointed to the one she'd indicated previously.

'Yes. Well…until we get to Adelaide. Then I'll be sitting up in the day-night seaters.'

'What? Why? You can't sleep in those things and then present at the conference on Monday.' He had a rather large cabin which had two beds.

Perhaps Dr Grainger might like to— He stopped his thoughts before they continued. It wasn't his place to solve the problems of the world, let alone the problems of petite and pretty Dr Grainger. He'd tried several times to take the world on his shoulders and had only ended up suffering from bouts of depression. No. It wasn't up to him to solve Euphemia's problems. Problems of a medical nature, problems where he could figure out a solution—that was completely different. It was one of the reasons he'd accepted the travelling fellowship because he'd needed to continue moving, doing something, *anything* so he didn't have to face his past.

'The seats aren't so bad,' Euphemia was saying, and Gil realised he'd zoned out for a moment. 'No worse than economy class in an aeroplane besides, I have friends joining me when the train stops in Adelaide so that way we can all be together.'

It wasn't his problem where she sat or why, he told himself again. 'Fair enough.' He nodded politely, deciding now was a good time to escape her unnerving presence. 'Well, I hope you'll be able to join me for a cup of tea at some point over the next few days. It's a long train journey and I'd relish the opportunity to sit and chat with you.'

'I'd like that. Uh…from a medical point of view, I mean,' she added quickly, just in case he thought she might want to chat about other things. 'Uh…not that talking to you about more general topics wouldn't be appreciated but—' She cut herself off and closed her eyes for a split second, wondering if she could make this moment any more difficult. She doubted it.

'I understand.' Gil held out his hand, being the ever-polite professor, and then wished he hadn't. He was still simmering deep down inside from the last time they'd touched. Why had he instigated another? He cleared his throat and called on all the professionalism he could muster. 'It was nice to meet you, Dr Grainger.'

'You too, Professor Fitzwilliam.'

'Gil.'

A shy smile touched her lips. 'Gil.' Once again they seemed caught up in time, their hands clasped, their gazes locked. She breathed in his name and tried not to sigh. 'Uh…er…' She shrugged, feeling a little self-conscious. 'My friends call me Phemie.'

'Phemie.' Gil nodded, still enchanted to find such an unusual name for such an unusual woman. He gave her hand an extra little squeeze before releasing it. 'I sincerely hope to see you around, Phemie Grainger.'

'Likewise, Gil Fitzwilliam.' With one more smile, he turned and walked away. She stood there like a gormless twit and watched him open the carriage door, heading through that one and then through to the previous carriage. There was no way she could help the deep, satisfied sigh that escaped her.

She'd just met Professor Fitzwilliam. *The* Professor Fitzwilliam. A man she'd admired for…well, since she'd been a medical student. He'd been writing medical articles for the *Journal of Emergency Medicine* for years and whenever her copy had arrived, his were the first articles she'd read.

Phemie returned to her cabin and sank into the chair. She looked at the notes for her presentation but found she simply couldn't concentrate. She was restless now and there was no-where to prowl in the small cabin.

She'd met Professor Fitzwilliam…*and* he'd invited her to call him Gil. Honestly, she was behaving like a schoolgirl meeting a film star for the first time. Awe-struck and completely irrational. She needed help. Back-up. She reached for her mobile phone and was pleased to discover there was coverage. She pressed the buttons for the pre-set number.

'Dr Clarkson.'

'Melissa? It's Phemie.'

'Bored already? Didn't we just put you on the train about an hour ago?' her good friend Melissa Clarkson asked. Melissa was an OB/GYN working at the clinic and hospital in the small outback town of Didjabrindagrogalon which covered the district and community Phemie and her colleagues serviced through the Royal Flying Doctor Service. The two women had been friends since Melissa had come to search for her brother, Dex, but had instead fallen in love with her brother's best friend, Joss. Now happily married, Melissa was well and truly settled in the outback and this only served to strengthen the friendship they shared.

'He's here.'

'Who's where?'

'Gil…uh, I mean Professor Fitzwilliam.'

'He's on the train?'

'Yes.'

'Going to the conference in Sydney?'

'Yes. I guess so.'

'Why is he on the train? I know he had a two-day stopover in Perth because Dex went and caught up with him there. I wonder why he didn't fly to Sydney?'

'Dex knows him? Like as a friend?' Phemie asked with mounting incredulity.

Melissa chuckled. 'Yes. The two of them worked together years ago on the Pacific island of Tarparnii. From what Dex said, Gil was quite involved with Pacific Medical Aid for a while.'

'Why didn't Dex tell me he knew Gil...uh, I mean Professor Fitzwilliam?' Phemie closed her eyes, unable to believe she was already starting to *think* of him in a more personal way. That wouldn't do. It wouldn't do at all. She had no room in her life for any new...people. She was full to bursting and Gil, uh, Professor Fitzwilliam would just have to remain on the outer rim.

'You know Dex. He's hardly the name-dropping type. Besides, he's been too busy falling in love with Iris. You should see the two of them. Ugh. I hope Joss and I didn't look that gushy when we first got together.'

Iris was the new paediatrician who had come to Didja for only six months but now that she and Dex had sorted out their differences and also because Iris had recently become guardian to the most gorgeous baby girl, the Didja clinic had scored itself a permanent paediatrician. Phemie sighed, thinking how nice it was that her friends were all finding their perfect mates, and that deep gnawing sensation of loneliness she worked hard to ignore started to raise its ugly head again.

'You did. Trust me. It was nauseating,' Phemie teased, needing to get her thoughts back on track.

'Oh. Well. Can't be helped,' Melissa brushed Phemie's teasing aside. 'So, tell me, why is it a big deal that Gil's on the train?'

'He asked me if I wanted to join him for a cup of tea,' she murmured.

'What? The fiend. How dare he? Oh, the impertinence of the English,' Melissa joked. 'Tea! Who would have thought?'

Phemie chuckled, already starting to feel less rattled. 'Stop.'

'So when are you joining him for this tea-drinking ritual? In the dead of night? Early morning? Oh, I know—at afternoon teatime? Seems perfect for the tea-drinking to be performed.'

'I don't know.' Phemie shook her head. 'It was just sort of an open-ended invitation. I don't know what to do. Do I accept? Do I ignore it?'

'He's rattled you,' Melissa stated. 'The unrattleable Phemie has been rattled.'

'Well…I…I…er…'

'You're stammering. You never stammer. Not unless you're well and truly rattled. Good grief, Pheme. What happened when you two met?'

'We sort of…bumped into each other. Literally.'

'Ooh.' Delight dripped from Melissa's tone. 'Do tell, girlfriend.'

Phemie gave Melissa a quick recount of the past fifteen minutes. 'I'm supposed to be concentrating on my paper, on getting everything sorted out in my head so I don't make a fool of myself when I get up in front of thousands of people on Monday to do my presentation.'

'And now you can't concentrate because of *him*?'

'Of course I can concentrate. That's why I called you. If I talk it all out, then I can put it aside and focus.'

'Oh, piffle. You have hours and hours of doing nothing on that train.'

'Anthony's getting on—'

'On Friday morning. It's Wednesday, Phemie,' Melissa pointed out. 'Look, there's more than enough time for you to go over the presentation, spend time with Anthony *and* have the occasional cup of tea with a medical genius. It's a three-day journey from Perth and perhaps Professor Fitz-yummy is looking for a bit of company. Professional and platonic, of course. He is a gentleman after all.'

'Yes.'

'A gentleman who has already held you in his arms—twice!'

Even though Melissa couldn't see her, Phemie coloured a little at her friend's words. 'It was the train. It was lurching,' she said defensively.

'You believe that if you need to. Phemie?'

'Yes?'

'Go and have a cup of tea with him. Talk about the latest medical breakthroughs or whatever it is that you find interesting but for goodness' sake, relax a little. Let yourself go. Step outside that very comfortable comfort zone you've locked yourself inside. It's all too easy to stay put.' Melissa's tone said she knew what she was talking about.

'I've taken steps outside my zone,' Phemie felt compelled to say, even though she knew her friend was right. 'I'm working in the middle of nowhere, for goodness' sake. I left Perth. I'm out in the wide brown land…well, ochre land at any rate, and I'm meeting new people. I think that qualifies as stepping outside my comfort zone.'

'Or perhaps it's simply doing the same moves inside a different shape. You're the nurturing type as well as a workaholic. Going to Sydney on the train should force you to do one thing—slow down. You're still taking care of everyone else's needs except your own.'

'And you think having a cup of tea with Professor Fitzwilliam will take care of my needs?'

'It might.'

'Must be pretty powerful tea, then.'

Melissa laughed. 'Just promise me you'll try and be open to new experiences.'

'Such as joining an esteemed English professor for tea?'

'Exactly.'

An hour later, Melissa's words still ringing in her ears, Phemie gave up on the pretence of reading and searched for her shoes. All passengers had been warned by the train stewards to always wear closed shoes when walking about the train—especially between carriages.

As she left her cabin, she realised the train was really rocking now and she wondered whether the drivers were trying to make up time. She made it to the next carriage, trying to ignore the blast of cool air as she'd stood on the gangplank that connected the two cars together. In just under a month, winter would be here. Not that that mattered much where she lived, about fifty kilometres outside Didja's town centre at the RFDS base. Even in winter, the weather was still rather warm.

She walked through the next carriage, then heaved open the heavy door at the end, crossing into another carriage which she realised was the lounge car. Several people were seated here and there, some talking quietly, some reading or doing work on their computers. She headed through, wanting to get to the dining carriage to at least get a warm drink, hoping that might help her to relax.

'It's full.' A deep English accent washed over her and she turned to find Professor Gilbert Fitzwilliam sitting at one of the corner lounges, a Thermos on the table in front of him.

'Oh, hi.' Why had her heart-rate picked up the instant she'd seen him? 'Pardon?'

'The dining carriage. It's completely filled with people.'

'Oh.' Euphemia frowned, then shrugged. 'Oh, well. I guess I'll have to wait until the rush is over for a warm drink.'

'Not necessarily.' Gil indicated his Thermos. 'Would you care to join me?' When she hesitated for a moment, he continued, 'After all, I *do* remember inviting you to join me at some point. That point could be now.'

Phemie smiled. 'Yes. Yes it could.' She remembered Melissa's encouraging words about taking a step outside her comfort zone. Besides, it wasn't as though Gil was a complete stranger. She already felt as though she knew him, thanks to his brilliant articles and textbooks, and Dex knew him so that gave her a personal connection of sorts and a reason to trust him a little sooner than she would have trusted the average stranger. Not that she was implying that he was average because, just by looking at him, she could tell he was more than above avera— She stopped her thoughts when she realised he was still waiting for an answer. 'Uh…well…all right, then, Professor. Let's do this now.' Phemie flicked the end of her blonde ponytail down her back and sat down opposite him.

'Excellent.' Gil opened the lid of his Thermos

and poured out a cup. 'I'm sorry if you take tea with milk or sugar. We could probably rustle some up from somewhere but I'm afraid I drink it black.'

'All the better to infuse your mouth with flavours?' she asked.

Gil chuckled and the warmth of the sound washed over her. 'Something like that.'

'Black is fine.' Phemie took a sip and tried not to make a face. 'What sort of tea is this?' She'd been expecting plain black, not slightly flavoured.

'Earl Grey. Don't like it?'

'It tastes like dishwater.'

'Is that so? Well, as I am not a connoisseur of dishwater, I can't cast a vote on your assessment. Do you drink it often? Dishwater, I mean.'

Phemie laughed. 'Can't say that I do, although where I live, running water is considered a luxury so if anything gets into our water tanks, it can taste pretty gross.'

'So you don't infuse your mouth with the flavours from the washing-up water?'

She shook her head and laughed again. He was handsome. He was polite and now he was bringing out humour. Lethal combination.

'Tell me, then, Dr Grainger, what sort of tea do you usually drink?'

'Australian, of course. It's rich, full bodied and there's plenty of it.'

The light in Gil's eyes twinkled as their gazes held. Was she not only describing the essence of Australia but the essence of Euphemia Grainger? 'I'm intrigued. Sounds like something I should experience whilst I'm in your country.'

'I think you should.' Why did she get the feeling they were having two completely different conversations? There was a light in his eyes, one that made her heart rate instantly increase.

'It's settled, then.'

'What is?' Confusion creased her brow.

'That you'll meet me in the conference hotel lobby at the end of the first day's sessions to treat me to a rich, full-bodied Australian experience.'

Was he still talking about tea? 'In Sydney?'

'They don't drink tea in Sydney?'

'Yes. Of course they do. Sorry.' She was still coming to terms with the fact that Gil was more than happy to spend time with her at the conference...in a personal capacity. 'I'm not sure I remember where a good tea house is in Sydney. It's been a while since I was there.'

The train jolted a little and Gil rocked forward towards her but there he stayed, his face close, his words a little more intimate than before. 'Then we shall have to explore together.'

Phemie held her breath, her gaze flicking to his mouth, then back to his eyes, a strange warmth settling over her. The moment grew more intense when Gil visually caressed her lips. Her heart started pounding wildly in her chest, not from fright or uncertainty but from pure attraction—such as she'd never felt before.

Her lips parted to allow the pent-up air to escape. On a personal level, she knew next to nothing about this man and he knew next to nothing about her, yet there seemed to be something new, something exciting brewing between them...and it wasn't the dishwater-tasting tea.

'Euphemia.' Her name was a caress on his lips and for one heart-stopping second she thought he might continue his journey towards her and actually kiss her. She closed her eyes, trying to control her thoughts, her breathing, but all she could think about was how, at this second in time, she wanted to be free, to let go, to break all the rules and regulations she'd previously set down for her life.

She *wanted* him to kiss her. *Wanted* to know what it would be like. *Wanted* to feel the touch of his mouth against hers. It was ludicrous. It was impossible. It was what she wanted.

The next thing she knew, there was a loud screeching noise and she was thrown to the floor, landing hard with a heavy thud. She could feel firm hands on her upper arms and then she was somehow hauled against firm male chest as they started to slide along the floor of the carriage.

The train was stopping—and it was stopping at a rapid rate.

CHAPTER TWO

PEOPLE were screaming, yelling. The scent of panic was in the air. A baby cried. The screeching noise continued. As the train came to a halt, all Phemie was conscious of was Gil and the way he'd automatically protected her, his body taking the brunt of the impact as they slid into the bolted-down lounge chairs opposite to where they'd previously been sitting.

When they finally stopped, it took a second for rational thought to return.

'Are you all right?' His voice was soft near her ear but full of concern.

'Hmm?' She opened her eyes, looking into those gorgeous brown depths which had hypnotised her earlier. She was lying in his arms, their bodies so close together she was positive he could hear her heart pounding wildly against her chest. The main question was whether it was pounding so badly due to the surprise of the train stopping or because she was in his arms?

'Euphemia!' His voice became louder and she saw the worried look in his eyes.

'Yes?'

'Are you hurt? Bruised? Can you stand?' As he spoke, he felt her head and down her arms. How could she—a trained medical professional—be more concerned with her reaction to this perfect stranger than the train accident? What was wrong with her?

'I'm fine.' And she wasn't sure she liked him touching her, simply because it caused a mass of tingles to flood her entire body and explode like fireworks. She shifted but it appeared he wasn't ready to move away just yet. 'I'm fine,' she reiterated. 'I'm OK. You? You hit that lounge pretty hard.'

Phemie touched his shoulder but on feeling the firm muscle realised her touch was anything but medical. Bad. It was bad. He was *Professor Gilbert Fitzwilliam*! She wasn't supposed to have an instant attraction to this man. He was a medical genius. He was a research phenomenon and he lived on the other side of the world. Apart from that, Phemie was most certainly not looking for any sort of romantic relationship. Not now. Not ever.

'I'll live.' Gil carefully stood, holding out a hand to help Phemie up. The sooner he put some distance between them the better. Having that gorgeous, petite body of hers pressed hard against his was something he hadn't expected to experience but now he had, he couldn't help his mounting intrigue for this woman.

Once she was on her feet, he let her go. Distance. He needed distance from her. He was so intent on moving away he almost stood on his Thermos, which had rolled to the floor. He quickly picked it up and placed it on a chair. 'Someone's pulled the emergency stop handle.'

'Agreed.' Phemie brushed herself down, straightening her clothes, pleased there was now space between them. She dragged in a few breaths to focus herself. 'Emergency stop means—'

'Something has gone wrong. No doubt medical assistance will be required.' He headed for the carriage door. 'I'll find a steward then hopefully we'll know what's going on. Stay here and ensure everyone in this carriage is all right.' With that, he opened the weighted door. Phemie watched him go, liking the way he walked—sure and firm and with purpose.

As soon as he was out of sight, her brain clicked immediately into medical mode and she went to help the other lounge-car passengers. There were

a few bumps, a few bruises and scratches but for
the most part everyone seemed fine, just very
shaken. One man was more concerned about his
computer than anything else. Everyone had questions but Phemie didn't have any answers.

She had just finished checking the pulse of a
three-year-old boy, snuggled into his mother's
arms, his cries having settled somewhat, when Gil
strode back into the carriage, two stewards and a
guard following him. One of the stewards carried
a large medical kit.

'Dr Grainger. You're needed. This way.' His tone
was as brisk as his strides and realising she was
seeing the *Professor* in all his professional glory,
Phemie excused herself from the young mother
and followed the men.

'Apparently, there's been an incident a few carriages down.' Gil spoke softly yet clearly as they
made their way through the empty dining carriage
towards the rear of the twenty-two-car-long train.
'One of the passengers had an accident walking
between two of the carriages. His mate was behind
him, saw it happen and ran back to pull the emergency stop.'

'Do we have any idea what sort of injury?'

Her voice was calm, clear and in control. Gil was

pleased. It appeared he had a doctor who was more than happy to assist in this emergency. He'd realised years ago that emergency medicine didn't suit every type of medical professional, but for him it provided variety and unique challenges and was something he thrived on...especially since June and Caitie. Gil shook his head. Now was definitely not the time to even think about his past.

'Lots of blood has been the main report.' Gil indicated to one of the stewards as they walked through to the next carriage and nodded, indicating the man should start his debrief now.

'Uh...yeah...right, Doc. We uh...just got a message through our radios...' he indicated the two-way communication device '...saying a man had hurt himself and there was a lot of blood.'

Phemie nodded, thinking through possible scenarios, but there were simply too many. 'Has anyone contacted the authorities? Sent for medical support?'

'Uh...I think the driver has notified the rail authority but I don't know about anything else.'

Phemie reached into the pocket of her jeans and pulled out her phone.

'It won't work here,' the guard said. 'We're in the middle of nowhere.'

'We're only about four hours out of Didja and *this*

is no ordinary phone.' She punched in a number and a moment later was connected. 'Hi, it's Phemie.' She paused. 'I *am* having a break, I promise, but there's been an accident on the train.' The guard was able to give her their exact co-ordinates and she passed this information on. 'Get the plane in the air. I'll forward more details when I have them. Over.' She replaced the phone in her pocket.

'Over?' A quizzical smile tipped Gil's lips as they continued their way through the train. 'Do you always end your phone calls like that?'

'Oh. Yeah. Bad habit. I'm used to talking on a UHF radio.'

'Really?' Gil continued to be intrigued by this woman. 'Who did you just call?'

'RFDS.' At his blank look, she remembered he was from overseas and quickly explained. 'Royal Flying Doctor Service. We're based just outside Didja.'

'Didja?'

'Didjabrindagrogalon. It's the outback town where I boarded the train.'

'You work at the RFDS?'

'Yes.'

Gil digested this information as they finally arrived at the carriage with the injured passenger. As they'd walked, the stewards and guard had been stopped several times by people wanting to know what was happening. Some people were crying, others were visibly shaken, some had slept through the entire thing. Gil, however, was busy processing the information about Phemie. If she worked for the RFDS, which he presumed provided emergency medical support to the farthest reaches of this vast country, it surely meant she was an experienced doctor with several years of training behind her. Yet she looked so young.

Harlan, the steward carrying the medical kit, walked behind them. 'It's just down here…' He pointed as the end of the carriage came into view. There were lots of people standing around, blocking the way.

'Excuse me.' Gil's voice carried the authority necessary to make people obey. They shuffled by the crowd to find one man slumped to the floor, his eyes wide, his hands tinged with blood, his body shaking, staring blankly.

Beside him were another two stewards, leaning over a man in his early twenties. One was at his head, talking to him, trying to keep him calm. The other was at the man's feet. The patient's right leg was elevated, a blood-soaked towel around the foot.

'I'm Dr Fitzwilliam. What's happened?' Again,

Gil's voice was clear and smooth. Phemie watched an expression of relief cross the steward's face. The cavalry was there and they were more than happy to back away.

'His toe's come off. His big toe!' The steward holding the towel was the first to speak, the words said with utter disbelief. 'He wasn't wearing closed shoes. He went between the carriages, the train lurched, his toe got caught and…and…saying this out loud makes me feel sick.'

'We tell the passengers,' Harlan said sternly, 'we tell them no flip-flops. No bare feet. We tell them all the time.'

'Yes.' Gil took the first-aid kit from Harlan, holding it open so Phemie could extract gloves. 'Thank you. Now isn't the time for chastisement or laying blame. The legalities can wait until later. The first priority is for the patient to be assessed. Harlan, you need to find the missing digit.'

'His toe's really come off?' Phemie had managed to manoeuvre herself around so she could take over from the young steward who was holding the towel. 'We need to find it.'

'Find the toe?' Now the young steward turned a nasty shade of pale.

'Believe it or not.' Harlan's voice was strong

and sure. 'This isn't the first time something like this has happened. Of course, the last time was almost twenty years ago and even though we found the missing toe, it was too late to reattach it.' He seemed to be the one with the strongest constitution amongst the railway staff present and Phemie knew Gil had been right to put him in charge of the search. 'I'll get that organised immediately.' He turned to the guard and started discussing exactly where they had stopped and how far back they would need to begin looking.

Gil crouched down near the friend who was against the wall but kept glancing to where Phemie was busy assessing the foot in question. He put the first-aid kit down where she could reach it, then focused on the injured man's friend. 'What's your name?'

'Paolo.'

'I'm Gil. What happened? Can you remember?'

'We were just walking between the carriages. We were heading to the dining hall and Kiefer stumbled. I don't know. The train just lurched and then Kiefer was screaming and there was blood everywhere around his foot and the...the...I was right near the door and then I saw the emergency stop handle and I just...I just pulled it. I...' Paolo shook his head. 'There was blood and…' He clamped a hand over his mouth.

'It's OK,' Gil reassured him. 'You did the right thing. Any delay in stopping the train means we may not find the toe.'

'Oh—' Paolo went as white as a sheet, looking like he was going to faint.

Gil urged the man's head forward and motioned for Harlan to come over. 'Get someone to stay with Paolo, please. I need to assist Dr Grainger.'

'She's a doctor?' Harlan was stunned. 'She looks so young.'

As he made his way to Kiefer, Gil was pleased he wasn't the only one who'd thought Phemie to be a lot younger than she looked. 'Hey, there, Kiefer,' he said to their patient. 'I'm Gil and this is Phemie. Are you allergic to anything?'

'No. No.' Kiefer shook his head. Gil searched in the first-aid kit, pleased to find a penlight torch. He checked Kiefer's pupils. 'Been drinking tonight? Taking any substances?' He checked the man's pupils.

Kiefer shook his head again.

'I need to know. I don't care what it is but I need to know otherwise it makes it more difficult for us to treat you.' Gil could smell the faint remnants of beer on the breath of both Paolo and his mate but he needed to hear it.

'Beer. Just beer.'

'How many?'

'Three. Maybe four. Not that many. We'd just got started. We got hungry.' Kiefer was in so much pain Gil was surprised he hadn't passed out but the alcohol would have been enough to take the edge off the trauma.

'All right. Good.' The first-aid kit was well stocked but unfortunately there was nothing stronger than over-the-counter pain medication. It would have to do for now. Gil sent a steward to get a cup of water.

'How does it look?' he asked quietly as he watched Phemie. She'd placed the foot onto a clean towel and was trying to clean and wash the wound site to afford them a better look.

'From what I can see, it's been cleanly severed. There is sufficient skin to enable reattachment. He's a good candidate. I've asked for some ice-packs and also for a container of ice for when we find the missing digit.'

'Optimism. I like that.'

'Good, because I have it in abundance.'

'Really?'

Their gazes met, his brown eyes rich and almost teasing. For a split second it was as though they were back in the lounge carriage. Just the two of them, their minds having one conversation, their bodies having another. Tension. Awareness. Questions. They were all there and as Phemie looked away, she made the attempt to clarify her statement. 'Well, where my patients are concerned, at any rate.'

'Like all good doctors should,' he returned. Why had she felt the need to clarify? Was she not usually optimistic in other areas of her life? Her personal life? If that was the case, it only piqued his curiosity further. In fact, ever since he'd first seen Euphemia Grainger his thoughts had been more captivated by her than anything else. This was definitely something new for him to ponder, given that his thoughts were always about his research, his next lot of speeches and presentations. Thinking about a woman? Having a woman occupy his thoughts? No. That was wrong.

The steward returned with the cup of water and Gil administered two analgesic painkillers, knowing the previously consumed alcohol in Kiefer's system wouldn't react to the pills. Until help arrived, there wasn't much else he or Phemie could do except make their patient as comfortable as possible and find that toe.

Gil performed Kiefer's observations and reported the findings to Phemie. 'He's as stable as we can get him.'

'Good. I'm ready to bandage this foot up now. Did you want to look before I do so?' she asked, shifting slightly to make room where there wasn't any. Now that she'd said the words, she wasn't sure she wanted him to come any closer. If he did, it would only bring them into tight contact with each other, given the walkways were barely big enough to fit two people through side by side let alone hip to hip with a patient lying on the floor before them.

Gil tried to shift through but short of moving Kiefer's body to the side, getting anywhere near the foot in question was going to have to wait. He shook his head. 'I can't get through. Just show me from there. I have good eyesight.'

Phemie unwrapped the foot from the clean towel she'd draped over it and angled it slightly so Gil could see. He was, after all, Professor Gilbert Fitzwilliam, the British surgeon who had basically written the manual for emergency medical procedures. Whilst he perused Kiefer's foot, Phemie perused him. To say he wasn't at all what she'd expected was a bit of an understatement. He was more down to earth, more…natural than she'd thought, but, then, she'd never really thought about him as a person in his own right.

'You've done well at debriding. Bandage away. The healthier we keep the area, the better the chance of successful reattachment.' At that, he turned to Harlan, remembering to check on the status. The steward was the lynchpin in this whole retrieval operation and he'd done a good job. Whilst Gil and Phemie had been tending to the patient, Harlan's communication radio had been working overtime. Staff were out searching for the digit, other stewards were attempting to keep passengers as calm as possible and Gil knew it was Harlan who had given the train manager the right words to say over the loudspeaker to inform the passengers of the situation.

'Ice-packs are on their way,' Harlan informed them. 'Sorry it's taken so long.'

'No need to apologise,' Gil replied. 'We whole-heartedly appreciate the assistance you've provided and thank you. You've been most obliging.'

'Very good, sir.' Harlan almost made a little bow. Phemie couldn't help but smile as she expertly finished off Kiefer's bandage. Gil really sounded like the professor when he spoke like that, all British with pomp and ceremony. She liked it and hoped it would serve as a reminder of who he really was. That way, she at least had a hope of keeping herself under better control.

Gil checked on Paolo and found him to be improving and more in possession of his faculties. Phemie began asking Kiefer the same basic questions again and whilst she knew he hadn't hit his head, the amount of shock his body was experiencing was extreme.

She pulled off her gloves and put them into a small rubbish bag Harlan handed her. 'I might give my people another call. See where they're up to.' She pulled her phone from her pocket.

'The bat phone again?'

Phemie's lips twitched at Gil's words. 'It's more effective than shining a big bright light in the sky.' The professor was not only gorgeous, affecting her in ways she didn't want to contemplate, but also had a wonderful sense of humour. He was just the type of man she should keep her distance from, starting with not agreeing to have tea with him in Sydney. She dialled the number of the Didja RFDS base and thankfully, Ben answered immediately.

'It's me. The emergency is a spontaneous amputation of the big toe. Right foot. We have people out looking for the toe. Patient is stable but requires analgesics. If you could contact Perth hospital, I think it's best if Sardi takes the patient directly rather than going through Didja.' She paused. 'Three hours. That's our window and we've already used half an hour.' Phemie listened. 'I'm fine. I have help. No, another doctor. Yes.' She turned her head, her gaze encompassing Gil. 'It was rather fortunate. Right, that's about it for now. Thanks, Ben.'

She finished the call and put her phone away. 'They should be here in about an hour, maybe less.'

'We're going to need more people searching for the toe.' Harlan had heard what she'd said and he called through to the train manager to inform him of the situation.

'The most obvious place would actually be on the tracks themselves,' Phemie said then shrugged. 'But who really knows. I've never had to look for a missing digit before.'

'First time for everything?' Gil asked as he started to perform Kiefer's observations.

'Have you had anything like this happen to you before?'

'On a train travelling across Australia?' he asked with a hint of mischief. 'No.'

Phemie simply smiled and checked on Paolo. The other man didn't want to leave his friend but Phemie managed to convince him to go and pack their things and get ready to leave the train. 'Kiefer's going to need your help. Your reassurance. Your support. Are you from Perth?' Paolo nodded and she continued, trying to get Paolo's thoughts into a position where he'd be more of a help than a hindrance. 'Then at least you'll have somewhere to stay.'

'So I need to pack our things?'

'The better prepared we are when the plane arrives, the better it will be for Kiefer,' she encouraged. Thankfully, Paolo now had a lot more colour in his face and was able to stand and walk quite easily back to his carriage to get things organised.

When he'd gone, Phemie looked at Gil. 'How's Kiefer doing?'

'Stable. Tell me, will the plane be able to land close to the train? I mean, there's no airstrip nearby, is there?'

Phemie smiled. 'For a start, we're on the tip of the Nullarbor Plains. There's *nothing* but the odd shrub here and there, and, secondly, we're alongside the main road. I was just about to ask Harlan to arrange for any traffic to be stopped so the plane can land.'

'That would be beneficial.' Gil nodded.

'Oh, you'd better believe it. There's nothing like making an emergency landing on a road when there are cars heading straight towards you, neither of you knowing which way to swerve.'

'Really?' Gil's eyes widened and Phemie's smile increased. 'Are you being serious, Dr Grainger?'

Harlan chuckled at her words and again lifted his radio to issue more orders. He certainly was 'point-man' and Phemie was exceptionally pleased they'd managed to get someone who was as good at his job as Harlan had proved to be.

'Excuse me, Doctors,' the steward said a few moments later. 'I'm receiving lots of reports of other people with injuries and problems due to the train stopping. I was wondering if—'

'Set up the lounge carriage as a treatment area.' Gil's tone was firm. 'Dr Grainger and I will see whoever has a complaint. If it's possible to find any other medical personnel on the train, their assistance would be invaluable.' Gil then pointed to their patient. 'Kiefer will need to be moved as well so we can continue to monitor him until the RFDS arrive.'

'Very good, Doctor,' Harlan replied, and again turned to talk into his radio, issuing orders.

'Ready for the next round of injuries?' Gil asked.

Phemie nodded, a smile in her voice as she spoke. 'Nothing like doing an emergency clinic on a stationary train in the middle of the outback.'

'I'd have thought you would be used to it. Doing clinics and providing treatment to people who are too far away from medical care.' Gil was intrigued, not only with her job but with the woman herself. He was looking forward to really seeing her in action, doing what she did best.

'I am, but I usually have a team I know and trust as well as quite a few more medical supplies than we have here.'

'Up for the challenge?' His dark eyes were alive with excitement.

Phemie watched him closely. 'You're enjoying this.'

'Not the fact that people are hurt,' Gil quickly pointed out. 'Never that, but the chance to do some real outback medicine? Yes.'

'You like new challenges,' she stated, pleased with her insight.

'What doctor doesn't?' he quipped, but she had the feeling he was playing down his delight at doing something different. As Kiefer was transferred to the stretcher and an announcement made asking for any trained medical personnel to report to the lounge carriage, Phemie continued to think about Gil and his excitement. She guessed that after travelling the world for a year, giving lectures and demonstrations, this sort of medicine *would* be different and challenging for him.

When they arrived at the lounge carriage, she once more performed Kiefer's observations and was pleased the man was still stable. There had been no report yet that they'd found the toe and she hoped sincerely it was indeed found before the plane was ready to transfer Kiefer to Perth.

'I have some medical helpers for you,' Harlan announced, and indicated the three people standing behind him. First, he introduced Gil and Phemie then pointed to a man in his forties. 'This is Julian, he's a registered nurse.' Julian shook hands with both Gil and Phemie.

'I usually work in geriatrics,' he informed them, 'but whatever you need, I'm more than willing to provide.'

'And I'm Wilma,' said a woman in her late sixties. 'I've been a retired triage sister for quite some time but that doesn't mean I've forgotten anything.'

'I don't doubt it.' Gil smiled at her.

'And this is my granddaughter Debbie.' Wilma indicated the young twenty-year-old next to her. 'She's a dental assistant and I thought she might be useful to help with any administration and minor bandaging.'

'I'm first-aid trained as well,' Debbie spoke up.

'Thank you for your offer of help.' Gil's smile was warm at all three. 'I've no idea how this is going to play out but we no doubt have a very long train filled with confused and scared people. Debbie, as your grandmother has suggested, if you're happy to organise the files and keep everyone happy, that would be very helpful. Wilma, you do triage? Anyone requiring immediate attention goes either directly to Phemie or myself. Julian, you take care of the patching-up jobs, Wilma helping you as and when you need it. If anyone has any concerns, please don't be afraid to ask. We're all strangers but we need to work as a team, to put people's minds at ease and to ensure their needs are met. I've asked Harlan to have his stewards bring those passengers who are asking for medical attention right to us rather than announcing we have a makeshift A and E set up.'

'That would just cause panic,' Phemie agreed.

'Debbie, you're going to have your hands full but everyone's details must be recorded before they're seen by any of us. I also believe a tea trolley is being organised in case people need fluids.'

'Remember,' Gil said as the door to the carriage opened, 'if you're not sure, ask questions. That way, we can attempt to avoid any unnecessary errors.' Three elderly patients were ushered through the door and Gil nodded. 'Let's get to work.'

For the next few minutes, the lounge car seemed to fill up quite quickly. Now that there was somewhere to bring people who were complaining of injury or stress, the stewards seemed to be sending the entire passenger manifest. Phemie made sure she kept a close eye on Kiefer, but his observations remained stable.

As they all treated patients, some with minor injuries, some requiring suturing, Phemie couldn't help but watch Gil, watch his techniques, the way his clever hands seemed to heal his patients simply by touch. He also had a wonderful bedside manner, making people of all ages feel completely at ease. He really was quite a man and it was an absolute honour to have the opportunity to really see him in action.

The other volunteer helpers, Julian, Wilma

and Debbie, were doing a marvellous job. The majority of people presented with cuts and bruises, most needing bandaging and reassurance.

Phemie was treating a heavily pregnant woman who had confessed she was travelling on the train because she was not permitted to fly.

'I just want you to check the baby. I fell quite hard when the train stopped and I don't know if everything—' She broke off, unable to finish her sentence. Phemie's heart went out to her. 'I know it's probably nothing but I just need to know the baby's all right.'

'Of course I'll check the baby. Besides, knowing the baby is fine may actually help you get some rest and that's what you really need to be doing. Off your feet, and resting. You have relaxing scenery to watch and you may find that you even doze off.'

Gil listened nearby as Phemie talked reassuringly to the pregnant mother. She certainly exhibited a natural caring ability, not only for this woman but for all the patients he'd seen her treat.

He wondered what the RFDS set-up was like, what situations and scenarios they dealt with on a regular basis. He was completely intrigued by it all.

Phemie was busy treating an elderly man for bruises and abrasions when she tilted her head to one side and listened, before calling to Gil, 'Here they are.'

'What?' Gil strained, listening so hard he thought his eardrums might burst. 'I can't hear anything.'

'The drone of the plane.'

He listened again. 'No. No drone.'

She shrugged. 'Guess I'm used to it.'

It was a whole two minutes later that he was able to hear the plane. 'I'll go greet the guys. You stay here,' she said as she stood, then stopped and put her hand across her mouth. 'Oh. Sorry. I keep forgetting who you are. Is that all right? Do you mind—?'

Gil smiled at her, a smile which had the ability to turn her legs to mush, and she instinctively put a hand to the wall to support her. 'It's fine, Phemie. I understand. This is your job. Just go.' The way she'd confessed to treating him like any other colleague was great. She wasn't fawning over him, she wasn't bowing and scraping to his every whim, as had happened during the past year that he'd been travelling.

He had his own support staff, including a secretary, events manager and personal aide. They all made sure he was where he was supposed to be and on time. Thankfully, they hadn't accompanied him on this train ride, instead preferring to fly across to Sydney to ensure everything was set up and ready for his arrival on Saturday.

Gil had no idea what this long delay would do to their overall timing but an emergency was an emergency. He would contact his staff when they stopped in Adelaide—the next city on their route. Until then, he was more than content to simply be a colleague of the delightful Euphemia Grainger. In fact, he wondered if he could somehow wangle an invitation to come and visit her Flying Doctor base once the conference was over.

He had a whole week set aside as 'vacation' time. His staff wanted to lounge about on Australia's famous golden beaches with little umbrella drinks in their hands. That wasn't for him. Going to a Flying Doctor base, doing something completely different, sounded like heaven. The more he dwelt on the idea, the more he liked it. Now all he had to do was get Phemie to agree.

When she eventually returned, it was with her colleagues and they were able to give Kiefer stronger analgesics, before they transferred him to the stretcher and prepared him for the plane.

'Still no sign of the toe?' Madge, the outback nurse practitioner, asked as they loaded Kiefer into the plane. Valma, the other nurse, was making sure Paolo was seated and the luggage stored. Gil had left their volunteer helpers to monitor the rest of the patients. There was no one urgent for him to treat and, besides, he wasn't about to miss seeing the RFDS in action.

'I was positive they'd find it.' Phemie couldn't believe she'd been wrong but looking for a severed toe along a railway line in the middle of such an enormous country really was like trying to find a needle in a haystack.

'They'll find it.' Gil put his hands on Phemie's shoulders and gave them a little squeeze. She tried hard to ignore the shock waves coursing through her system. It was ridiculous that a man she'd just met could evoke such a reaction yet that was exactly what was happening. She schooled her thoughts and attempted to keep herself as aloof as possible even though he was still touching her. 'Keep that optimism alive, Dr Grainger.'

His voice was rich and deep and its magnificence passed from the top of her hair to the tips of her toes. She tried not to close her eyes at the way he was so intimately affecting her. 'B-but the plane's about to leave.'

'And they'll—'

'Gil! Phemie!' It was Harlan. He was running

towards them, holding a plastic lunchbox in his hands. 'We've found it. We've found it!'

'There you go, Phemie. See? Your optimism was right.' Gil gave her shoulders the briefest of squeezes before he dropped his hands and raced over to meet Harlan. He checked inside the container and found the severed digit on ice. 'Ready for transplant,' he announced triumphantly as he handed it to one of the RFDS nurses.

'Let's get in the air,' Sardi ordered as she headed for the cockpit. 'Knock 'em into a pile of dead bones at the conference,' Sardi called over her shoulder to Phemie.

'She means knock 'em dead,' Phemie explained to Gil as she watched her colleagues prepare for take-off. She herself had done it a thousand times before, ensuring the patient was stable, closing the doors, making sure everything was locked and in place. 'Sardi sometimes gets her English phrases mixed up.'

'A female pilot?' Gil was impressed.

'Sardi's the best.'

'Good to hear. Are there any males working at your base?'

'Ben does a lot of the administration. He's a nurse as well but so far he's the only bloke.'

'Lucky Ben. Surrounded by beautiful women all day long.'

Phemie could feel Gil's gaze on her and forced a nervous laugh. Surely he couldn't mean that *she* was beautiful? Sure, she knew she was OK looking but she'd hardly call herself beautiful. Small. Tiny. Petite even, but never beautiful.

They all moved right out of the way, waiting for the plane to taxi and take off. 'I don't think Ben sees it that way. I think he goes around the twist being surrounded by females all day long. Plus, he and his wife have three girls so there's really no hope for him.'

'Do you think Ben would like to have another man around next week?'

'I think he'd be delighted,' she said, thinking of the part-time medic position which had been advertised yet again. Trying to get doctors to come to the outback was nigh on impossible yet so desperately needed in a country the size of Australia. 'If there was another man around, poor Ben might finally be able to win the argument of whether or not the toilet seat remains up or down!'

'Then I accept.'

Phemie blinked twice then frowned, looking up at Gil. 'You accept what?'

'The position.'

'The position of what?' She was now totally perplexed. 'Gil, what are you talking about?' They turned and headed back towards the train.

'The position of visiting medical doctor for the week after the conference.'

CHAPTER THREE

'WHAT?'

Phemie was so startled by his words that she misjudged the depth of the uneven ground and came crashing down. Gil was by her side in an instant, helping her to her feet, even though she was trying to push him away at the same time.

'I'm fine. I'm fine.' She brushed herself down, knowing the reddish dust would never completely come out of her pale green top. Thankfully, her jeans were dark enough not to stain. She didn't want to feel his hands on her or his arms around her or to have his firm muscled chest anywhere near her own. His light spicy scent was addictive and the way the lightest touch of his hand on her body sent her insides spiralling out of control was something she'd rather not have to deal with right now.

She had a paper to present at the conference in Sydney. She had her brother and his friends joining her on the train when they reached

Adelaide. She'd just had to watch her colleagues fly off without her and all of it combined was making her rather vulnerable. There was too much going on in her life right now and the last thing, the very last thing she needed was to hear Professor Gilbert Fitzwilliam declare he would be accompanying her back to the RFDS base for one week after the conference! No. It would not do.

Of course, on a medical level, everyone would be delighted to welcome him to their base. They'd be keen to have someone of his qualification and expertise helping out with the various emergencies and clinics.

But to have him simply declare his intention had knocked Phemie for six. Even now, as they walked back to the train, she was completely aware of him. She could feel him watching her every step lest she should stumble again.

She was not a damsel in distress. Far from it. She'd looked after herself for years, holding her family together as she and her parents had dealt with the differences and difficulties her younger brother Anthony experienced. Now Anthony was living independently in an assisted facility in Perth, travelling to Adelaide for holidays, and soon he would catch the train to take him to the opposite side of the country from where he'd lived. Her parents were enjoying their first holiday alone since their honeymoon. And Phemie? Phemie had left home, too. She'd moved to the middle of nowhere to work with the RFDS and had found the outback the most glorious place in the world.

No. She was not a damsel in distress, neither was she a fool. She refused Gil's help as they climbed back onto the train but even as she hoisted herself up, she knew she couldn't turn down Gil's other offer—that of visiting their base for a week after the conference.

She could certainly understand why he would want to view the whole RFDS set-up. He was from another country, one where they obviously didn't cover so much territory, given that England itself could fit nineteen times inside the State of Western Australia. The RFDS was unique and it was only right that an A and E specialist such as Professor Gilbert Fitzwilliam would want to see such a place in action.

Although, she pondered, it didn't necessarily have to be her own base where he spent his time. That thought sparked another and the idea grew.

That's what she would do. When she arrived in Sydney, she would call the Australian director of the RFDS and suggest that Professor Fitzwilliam be assigned to one or the other bases. The one stationed near Katherine in the Northern Territory might be good for Gil to observe, given they were certainly busy almost every day of the year. They covered a lot more territory than the Didja crew and he might even have the opportunity to visit her friends Sebastian and Dannyella at Dingo Creek. Yes. He could go there. The real heart of the outback…which was far away from her.

'So? What do you think?' Gil asked as they headed back through the train, leaving Harlan to take care of the clean-up and other official duties. Harlan had also told them he'd need to have an accident report filled in but it could be done later.

'Think of what?' Phemie played for time, purposely ignoring him. Why was her heart thumping a little too fast against her chest? Was it due to Gil's nearness or because she was about to defy him? They made their way through the carriages, back towards the lounge car.

'Of me coming to the RFDS base?' Gil's eyes were alight with fun and excitement and for one brief, blinding moment Phemie *wanted* him to come back to the Didja Base with her. She didn't want to send him anywhere else, not when he looked at her like that.

She could well imagine the two of them, sitting on the front porch at the base, looking up at the stars as she pointed out the different constellations in the southern hemisphere. They would rock on the rocking chairs, they'd relax and chat after a busy day travelling either to a clinic or an emergency. He'd look at her with that gorgeous smile he was giving her now and she would capitulate and end up in his arms, his mouth pressed firmly to—

It was a bad idea. If her thoughts were this distracted by him after only a few hours in his presence, how on earth would she cope with him staying at the base, staying at *her* place, given that she lived at the base? No. It wouldn't do at all. The man had too much of a devastating effect on her equilibrium. Much better to see if he could go to Katherine for a visit. Much safer. He'd see more of the outback and he'd also be a three-day drive from where she was situated. Better.

His smile slipped a little, concern touching those deep brown eyes of his…eyes she could well and truly drown in. 'Are you all right, Euphemia?'

'Uh…I'm, er…I'm fine. Thanks.' She stammered quickly, fumbling over her words, not wanting him to guess the path her thoughts had taken. 'I have a lot on my mind. The conference, my paper, what's just happened with Kiefer. Uh…but with regard to you observing a—'

'Helping,' he interrupted. 'I don't plan to simply observe. I intend to be of service and work for my keep, so to speak.'

'Well…good. It does get busy and I'm sure your help would be greatly appreciated, but I'll need to see what I can organise. I'm not in a position to invite people back to the base to help out. There's a lot of paper work involved.'

'When isn't there?' he mumbled, but nodded as though he completely understood.

'I just can't make any promises. At this stage.' And that sounded to her own ears as though she was more than happy to have him around. Honestly, it seemed every time she opened her mouth, she just dug herself in deeper.

'That seems fair and I know you'll do your absolute best. You're a natural giver and carer, Phemie, and you go out of your way to help people. I know you'll put a lot of effort into doing all you can to assist me in my request.'

He wasn't being pompous, even though he might have sounded it. Phemie watched him as they headed back to their makeshift A and E and knew his words were sincere and from the heart. The brightness in his eyes also let her know he was serious and very interested in how the RFDS worked. She should be honoured that a man such as the professor would want to come all the way to the outback to not only see what they did but help out as well. Utilising someone with his skills and knowledge would be something she knew her boss wouldn't turn down, but on a personal note Phemie wasn't sure it was a good idea. Gil was just too…close for comfort.

When they returned to the lounge carriage, it was to find the number of waiting patients had dwindled.

'Most people were concerned about minor things and just wanted reassurance,' Wilma said as she made a cup of sweet tea for a patient. She handed over the tea and then pointed to where Julian was busy checking an elderly woman's pulse rate. 'Debbie's kept lists and files on everyone and has been highly effective in keeping people calm until they could receive treatment.' Wilma paused for breath. 'Kiefer and his friend are away, then?'

'On their way to Perth.' Gil confirmed. 'With the toe.'

'I'd heard it had been found. That's wonderful news.' The retired nurse beamed from ear to ear. 'Now, if the two of you would like to see those last few patients who have just come in, I think afterwards you should go and rest. Debbie and I can stay on here for the next few hours in case other people are brought in, and if we need you, we'll come and get you.'

Gil nodded but smiled at the other woman. 'Spoken like an experienced nursing sister who's used to bossing doctors around.'

Phemie chuckled as she'd been thinking the same thing. Not that she minded. Wilma had obviously been good at her job as today's organisation had shown and, besides, if she herself was able to escape to the confines of her cabin, to put some much-needed distance between herself and Gil, who was she to argue?

They treated the last few patients and as Phemie tidied up the rubbish and put it in the bin, she felt rather than saw Gil come to stand behind her. She turned to find he was wearing that delicious smile she liked and with it came the powerful effects. Phemie crossed her arms over her chest in an effort to give herself some sort of barrier against his natural magnetism. She was about to excuse herself when the loudspeaker above them crackled, startling Phemie a little.

'A little jumpy,' Gil noted. 'Are you usually so inclined?' He quirked an eyebrow, watching her with interest.

Phemie shrugged her shoulders then listened intently to what Harlan was announcing over the train's intercom.

'Would all passengers not presently receiving medical attention please return to their designated seats. Stewards will be around shortly to check on all guests.'

'Sounds as though we'll be getting under way soon enough.' Gil collected his Thermos from where it had been placed out of the way. 'I would be honoured if you allowed me to escort you back to your cabin.' He indicated the door not far from where they were standing and then made a small sweeping bow. 'After you, milady.'

Phemie couldn't help but smile. The man really was an odd mixture of old-world charm and dictatorial perfection. With the lift of an eyebrow he could either make someone shrink to the size of a peanut as he looked down that perfect nose of his or he could make a woman feel as though she were the most important person in the world, his eyes radiating his pleasure. Thankfully, she was experiencing the latter, those rich brown pools creating havoc within her.

Gil's smile increased when Phemie didn't move. She simply stood there, smiling up at him, her blue eyes bright with tired happiness. It was an unguarded moment, where her heart was there for him to see. He'd become quite good at reading people, especially with all the travelling he'd done that year, and as he looked into her eyes, he saw that there was a lot more to Phemie Grainger than he'd first thought.

He saw hardship, experiences, pain. He'd noticed it the first time he'd looked into her amazing eyes. They really were the window to her soul and he couldn't help but be intrigued by guessing what events had touched her life to make her look so tired yet so happy.

Life could be unkind. He knew all too well about that. He'd had a loving wife. He'd had a gorgeous child and both had been ripped from him. He'd known the pain of wanting what you couldn't have, what it was no longer humanly possible to have, and when he'd been unable to cope with the grief, with the agony of not being able to hold those he loved close to his heart, he'd locked himself away in the world of research and only recently had he actually started taking steps outside.

There was no way he wanted a romantic commitment ever again. He'd tried that once and he knew his heart wouldn't be able to take the pain and mortification in the event that something went wrong—again. Work had been his saving grace. Work had seen him through the dark nights and the depression, and now, after four years of constant work and concentration, he was starting to look outside those parameters.

Asking Euphemia to arrange for him to see a working RFDS base was still definitely within the bounds of his research, within the bounds of 'work', but it was something he wouldn't have asked a virtual stranger to do two years ago. He would have kept to his timetable. He wouldn't have deviated from the plan even for a second. Even taking the train from Perth across to Sydney had been his idea, not his handlers'.

This was the last stop on his world tour. He'd loved New Zealand and he'd been blown away by the few sights he'd seen when he'd spoken first in Brisbane, then in Darwin before making his way across to Perth. Still, apart from this train journey, he'd basically seen either the inside of a hotel room or a hospital operating suite where he'd lectured whilst performing surgery.

The train, which took three full days to snake its way across the wide brown land, had sounded like sheer luxury, especially when the rest of his team had declared they'd rather fly, something Gil preferred not to do, if at all possible. Too many planes. Too many flights. No. This time the train was a much better option. Three full days to simply be himself. To sit back, chat with the locals and absorb the quiet of a country half a world away from his own.

No one would know who he really was. No one would be pestering him to discuss his latest techniques. He'd just be a regular guy, travelling on a train, relaxing. Then he'd bumped into Phemie—literally. The fact that she'd recognised him almost instantly had been enough to burst his bubble but now he was sincerely pleased it had. He was having a much better time on this trip than even he'd been able to anticipate. Of course, attending to Kiefer and helping other passengers could, in no way, be classified as a good time, but watching Phemie work, observing her quick mind, assisting her—it had all been fantastic.

It was also fantastic to have her smiling at him

as she was now. Why was it that whenever it was just the two of them, like this, time appeared to stand still? Scientifically he knew it was a complete impossibility but emotionally it was delightful. To be able to glimpse those emotions again. To be able to feel the warmth of a woman's interested gaze. To have a moment to feel as though he'd stepped into the sunshine.

It was safe. It was simply a bubble and bubbles popped, forcing him back into the reality where life was structured and full of problems ready to challenge his mind into solving them. It was why he could allow himself to enjoy the way he felt in her presence because he knew, ultimately, the bubble would burst when they arrived in Sydney. Euphemia Grainger was simply a diversion. Something with a little extra spark to get him through that final leg of his tour.

'Phemie?' The instant he spoke, Phemie's expression changed, the smile slipping from her face. They'd probably been standing there for only a few seconds but for some reason it felt like much longer—for both of them if her reaction was anything to go by.

What had she been thinking? The thought wouldn't remove itself as they said thank you to

Wilma, Debbie and Julian then headed back through to the sleeping carriages. Had she been standing there wondering about how to pull some strings and get him onto her RFDS base? Had she been thinking about him in a professional capacity? What it might be like to have the 'famous' Professor Fitzwilliam at her small informal base? Would she worry about a thing like that? Or perhaps…just perhaps she'd been thinking about him in a more personal way?

Was she aware of the slight buzz which seemed to exist whenever they were alone together? He certainly was. He'd only met her a few short hours ago and on several occasions he'd found himself wondering what it might be like to capture her mouth with his, to hold her close and feel that soft petite body pressed against him.

It was wrong. It was ridiculous and it was something which would never happen. He was a man who not only prided himself on excellent self-control but who also knew that relationships were not for him. Add to everything that he and Phemie lived on opposites sides of the globe and there was a definite probability there would never be anything except professional courtesy or perhaps—at a stretch—friendship between them.

'This is me.'

Phemie stopped so suddenly Gil almost bumped into her. Just as well the train hadn't been moving or he would have once more found his arms sliding around her waist as he steadied them both. She was pointing at a cabin door.

'Ah…yes. I remember.'

Phemie smiled politely. 'Well…it's my cabin, at least for now.'

'And then the day/night seaters. You have friends joining you?'

'Uh…yes. My brother, actually. He and some friends are joining the train when we stop in Adelaide.'

'Your brother.' Now, why did he feel so pleased at that piece of information? 'The one who says the word "stuff" like water.'

'That's the one.' There was a small smile on her lips and she nodded. It was obvious she was very close to her brother and that was great. As Gil had been raised an only child, he'd often envied people who had close sibling and familial relationships.

'Well, I guess I should let you get to your own cabin. Here's hoping there are no other emergencies between here and Sydney.'

'Agreed.' He smiled and inclined his head politely. 'Goodnight, Euphemia. Sleep sweet.'

'Thank you.' He was so intent, so charming as he bade her farewell that she half expected him to gallantly raise her hand to his lips and kiss it. He didn't, however, and she opened her cabin door, slipping inside and leaning on it to ensure it closed properly.

What on earth was wrong with her?

Her heart was pounding against her chest. She was out of breath. Her knees were weak and her palms were perspiring. The man certainly had a killer smile and the way he smelt was utterly delicious and he was smart and handsome and had the most hypnotic eyes and deep, vibrating voice and she liked everything about him.

What on earth was wrong with her?

When the train finally pulled into Adelaide, Phemie was up, dressed and had already moved her bags to her appointed seat in the day-night section. She exited onto the platform, knowing they had a whole hour there before needing to board again.

She looked around at families greeting one another with hugs, kisses and tears of joy. There was no sign of Anthony and his friends. Phemie frowned, deciding to check inside the terminal in case they were waiting there, although she could have sworn they would have been waiting on the platform to see the train pull in. Slight alarm started to rise within her but she damped it down.

Inside the terminal, she walked the length of it, checking they weren't in the restaurant or in the little souvenir shop. No sign of them. Her mental alarm bells started to ring with more prominence. She pulled her mobile phone from her pocket and immediately hit the speed-dial for Liz's phone. While it rang, her gaze continued to search the terminal for any signs of Anthony or his friends. Had they been in an accident? Had someone gone missing?

As Liz's phone continued to ring, Phemie's intense alarm turned to panic.

'Good morning,' a deep voice said from behind her. She instantly recognised the British enunciation as Gil's and turned to look up at him. His eyes were still as powerful as ever. His voice was still as smooth. His nearness was still evoking a powerful reaction within her but everything was overshadowed by concern for her brother. 'I thought, if you're not busy, we might have breakfast—' He stopped when he saw the phone at her ear and the look of panic on her face. 'Good heavens, Phemie. Is everything all right?'

'I can't find my brother.'

'Oh. Where were you supposed to meet?'

'Here. On the platform or around it or…there was nothing firm but I'd expected him to be here when the train pulled in. He loves trains.' She was still looking around as she spoke, every muscle in her body tense, her voice strained.

Gil frowned a little. 'How old is he?'

'Twenty-four.'

Gil raised his eyebrows in surprise but quickly changed his expression back to neutral. If Phemie was older than her brother then she had to be either in her late twenties or early thirties. Good heavens, the woman certainly carried her age well.

'He's late. Anthony's never late.'

'I'm sure it's nothing to worry about.' Especially given her brother seemed old enough to look after himself. At twenty-four and travelling with friends, there was no telling where the young men might be and they were no doubt running behind schedule that morning due to late night partying.

'I can't get hold of Liz. Why isn't she answering her phone?' Phemie could hear her voice rising with mounting anxiety.

'Come. Sit down.' She was obviously agitated and he wanted to help in any way he could. He placed his hand beneath her elbow and was pleased when she allowed him to lead her to a chair by the door. She sat, cancelling the call she was making and trying another number.

'Why isn't he picking up?' She let it ring a few more times before hanging up. She clutched the phone between both her hands, her gaze intent on the door before it flicked around the terminal, desperate to have her brother miraculously appear before her.

'Maybe he forgot to charge his phone?' Gil offered the excuse in order to help. 'Batteries can go dead and usually when you're travelling you often forget to recharge them. I speak from experience on that point.'

'No doubt.' She wasn't really listening to him and he could see that not being able to find her brother was leading her into a greater state of anxiety. Gil was doing his best to try and calm her down.

'He'll be here.'

'He wanted to see the train pull in. He'll be so disappointed he missed it. He's been talking about it for months.'

Gil frowned. It was just a train, pulling into a

station. There was nothing exciting about that. Well, perhaps to a young boy, maybe but not to a twenty-four-year-old. Then again, perhaps Anthony was a train enthusiast or was simply a young man who liked trains. Who was he to judge?

She flicked open her phone and pressed another few buttons before holding it to her ear. 'If I can just get hold of Liz and find out what's—' The terminal doors swooshed open and Phemie was instantly on her feet. 'Anthony!'

She snapped her phone back into place as her feet took flight. She ran across the room and threw her arms around a man of about five feet five inches, who was a little portly around the middle and had the distinctive facial features of a person with Down's syndrome.

As Gil watched, Phemie's previous agitation now made complete sense. It was clear to all and sundry that she cared and loved her brother very deeply and he found himself once more re-evaluating the way he viewed Euphemia Grainger.

She really was becoming the most intriguing woman he'd met in an extremely long time and that fact in itself was dangerous.

CHAPTER FOUR

GIL didn't see either Phemie or her brother until that evening when he met them in the dining carriage. Euphemia had introduced him to Anthony in the train terminal and, of course, that meant he'd had to meet all of Anthony's friends and their carer—Liz.

Gil had been incredibly impressed that this group of adults, all with Down's syndrome, were travelling and exploring their own country. For people without a disability, sometimes the idea of stepping outside their comfort zone was something so terrifying they never even tried it and yet to see them openly embracing something new, something different and enjoying themselves really warmed his heart.

'I want to go to London one day and do lots of stuff,' Anthony had confessed when Phemie had explained that Gil was from England and that was why he 'talked funny', as Anthony had termed it. 'Mum and Dad have gone, haven't they, Phemie? They're doing heaps of cool stuff, aren't they, Phemie?'

'They are. They're cruising in Europe,' she supplied for Gil's sake.

'They send me postcards and stuff. I sent them postcards, too. I sent Phemie a postcard, too. I chose it all by myself and posted it in Adelaide.'

'Very clever,' Gil praised. 'I'm sure you picked just the right one for your big sister.'

'It had flowers on it and other pretty stuff. Phemie likes flowers, don't you, Phemie?'

'I do.' She'd kissed Anthony's cheek and smiled lovingly at him. Gil couldn't help the pang of envy that passed through him. He'd been raised by nannies and strict boarding-school masters, his parents more intent on their careers than on him.

He'd left them then, heading out of the station to stretch his legs whilst Phemie and Liz settled Anthony and his friends in for the next part of their journey. Gil was thankful he had the ability to be quite attentive to what was going on around him while indulging in a daydream. It wasn't something he'd done since his senior school days when he'd wished himself anywhere but at boarding school.

Today, however, he'd found himself thinking

about Phemie. What type of woman worked in the outback of a vast country? What type of woman rearranged her schedule to accommodate her brother, even if it meant she ended up exhausted before presenting at a medical conference? What type of woman had the ability to look into his eyes and make him feel as though his life was simply a shell of an existence?

He knew he'd locked himself away when June and Caitie had been cruelly ripped from his life in that plane crash but he'd always thought he'd hid it well. Phemie would have no idea what had happened in his personal life yet she had the ability to look at him and make him want more.

That wasn't going to happen. He didn't do *more*. He'd tried to have a normal life. He'd met a woman, married her, settled down, become a father to a gorgeous baby girl and it had all been cruelly snatched from him. He'd tried it and it hadn't worked. No. He didn't do *more*.

Gil stopped by the dining table where Phemie was cutting food into smaller pieces.

'Phemie's doing my food,' Anthony said proudly. 'She does it the best. Mum does it next best and Dad does it bestest after that. Liz doesn't do it best at all.' The last was spoken in a sort of stage whisper yet Anthony's volume still radiated quite clearly.

'And what about you?' Phemie prompted. 'How good are you at preparing your own food?'

'I am the king at doing my food and lots of other stuff but I like it when Phemie does it because she does it best. It's good stuff.'

Gil smiled at the young man and watched as Phemie finished what she was doing. 'It does appear your big sister knows exactly how you like your food,' Gil commented, then looked around. 'Where are your friends, Anthony?'

'I was first,' Anthony replied with a mouth half-full, and received a scolding from his sister. 'Sorry, Phemie,' he replied, then swallowed. 'I was first,' he repeated.

'They're all on their way here,' she supplied, and pointed to the empty diners' counter. 'So if you want to order something to eat, now would be the best time to do it.'

'Good to know.' Still Gil didn't move. He also noticed that Phemie didn't have any food in front of her. 'Have you already eaten? Can I get you something?'

'I'm fine. I'm not that hungry.'

'I can get you a cup of tea,' he offered, and

Phemie smiled politely. 'I'm sure they have a rich-bodied Australian tea.' He couldn't help but punc-tuate his words with a quick wink. The instant he'd done it, he silently scolded himself. What was he doing? Was he flirting with her? In front of her brother? In front of a carriage of other pas-sengers? It was so unlike him yet the instant she smiled at him he felt as though he'd been rewarded. She'd allowed him to continue sharing their private joke.

'Thank you, Gil, but I'm fine.' She paused for a moment, teasing confusion peppering her brow. 'Don't tell me you've actually drunk the tea they serve here? I thought you were Thermos man with your Earl Grey?'

Gil's smile was bright and natural as he nodded. 'My dishwater, you mean.' He received a chuckle from her. 'You're absolutely right, Phemie. I am very particular about my tea. I do like it just—so.'

Gil glanced at Anthony and then looked back to Phemie, his tone dropping a notch. 'What about later this evening? We could meet in the lounge car again and this time try to make it through a conversation without anyone else pulling the emergency cord.'

'Never, never pull the emergency cord,' Anthony chimed in.

'Mouth full,' Phemie pointed out, and he quickly mumbled an apology before swallowing. 'Uh...I think I'm going to be rather busy tonight so I'll have to pass.'

Gil nodded. 'Then our date for tea at the end of the first day's session must stand.'

Phemie wasn't too sure how wise it would be to continue any sort of personal relationship with Gil once they disembarked. On the train, it was as though they were in some sort of stasis where the rest of the world and the rules that surrounded it didn't apply. They were simply doctors, doctors who had worked together to help people. They were two people who seemed to have some sort of crazy gravitational pull towards each other. They were equals—and she knew once they arrived in Sydney and went their separate ways, everything would change. As it should. He was Professor Gilbert Fitzwilliam and she was an outback emergency doctor.

He lived in London, in the middle of one of the world's busiest cities. She lived on an RFDS base in the middle of nowhere. It gave a whole new meaning to 'worlds apart'.

At the moment, however, she felt crowded, confused and conscious that Anthony was paying them a lot of attention. He might not completely understand what they were saying and why, but she'd learned of old not to underestimate him. The last thing she needed right now was to try and explain her relationship with Gil to her brother. The fact that *she* didn't understand her relationship with Gil only made the situation more puzzling.

'Sounds great,' she agreed—anything to get him to leave.

'Excellent.' The train carriage door opened and all of Anthony's friends came traipsing in, bringing noise with them.

'I was first,' Anthony called, this time remembering to swallow his mouthful of food before speaking. He looked at Phemie and received praise for his actions.

Gil looked from Phemie to Anthony to the plethora of people who had just entered the dining carriage and then back at Phemie. He nodded politely. 'I'll leave you to it, then.'

'Thanks. Have a good evening,' she said, unable to look away as he left the carriage. Gil smiled at Anthony's friends and nodded to Liz as he shuffled past them. Phemie's gaze travelled over his broad firm shoulders, his straight back, his muscled thighs and tried not to recall how incredible it had felt to have that gorgeous body

pressed to her own. The sigh that escaped her lips
was unintentional.

'Now, that's a sizzling look,' Liz pointed out,
sitting next to Anthony. 'That man is pure sex on
legs, Phemie. Why on earth aren't you following
him out of here?'

'What's sex on legs?' Anthony asked and
Phemie glared at Liz, who only laughed in return.

'All I'm saying is that I wouldn't kick him out
if—'

'I get the picture.' Phemie held up her hands, indicating she wanted the present topic to end. She
focused on her brother. 'Would you like something else to eat, love?' She needed normalcy, not
ideas put in her head with regard to Gil
Fitzwilliam. The man may indeed be sex on legs,
as Liz had said, but that was beside the point.

No matter how sexy any man was, no matter
how he might make her feel, no matter how her
thoughts and body went haywire when he was
around, it would all be meaningless in the end.
Long-term relationships weren't for her. Marriage
wasn't for her. Having her own children was something she could never do.

Whilst she loved and adored her brother completely, there was no way she was going to risk

becoming pregnant and giving birth to a child with Down's syndrome. After Anthony had been born, her mother had looked further into Down's syndrome and discovered she was a carrier of the translocation trisomy 21 chromosome. This defective chromosome usually related to children being born with Down's. Her parents had both been tested and so had Phemie. It wasn't until she had been older and in medical school that her parents had told her she, too, was a carrier of the defective chromosome. There was an increased risk Phemie would give birth to a child with Down's syndrome. No way was she going to subject an innocent child to a life like that and even though she hated to admit it, she couldn't be a parent to a child with a disability.

She'd lived that life. She'd watched her parents for years, their long-suffering patience almost running out on several occasions. The way they hadn't been able to pay the proper attention to her because of Anthony, the way they'd had to rely on her to take up the slack. Phemie felt as though she'd aged prematurely, especially throughout her teenage years when her mother had undergone treatment for ovarian cancer. Her father had almost fallen apart, his soul being slowly destroyed each time her mother had needed another dose of chemotherapy or a blood transfusion. Anthony's care had fallen to her and as such, she'd never experienced the normal teenage things. There had been no time for parties, no time for experimenting, no time for boyfriends. She'd been a surrogate mother to her sibling.

Thankfully, the chemotherapy had worked and her mother was now in very good health, but those years had taken their toll on Phemie. She loved her family, more than anything and if she'd had to do it all over again, she would, but there were still traces of resentment flowing through her veins. She'd vowed never to put a child of her own through what she'd been through and the only way to ensure that never happened was never to have children.

Caring for others was what she was good at and that was what she was busy doing. Working in the outback, caring for the community, helping others in any way she could. Those were the choices she'd made and she was determined to stick to them. The emotions Gil Fitzwilliam evoked deep within her could mean nothing to her.

Phemie helped Anthony and his friends for the rest of the evening, ensuring everyone was in the right seat and comfortable when it was time to turn out the lights and go to sleep.

She and Liz chatted quietly for a while, though fatigue claimed her friend and soon Phemie found herself sitting in a carriage full of sleeping people, yet she herself was wide awake…awake and, for some strange reason, unable to stop thinking about Gil.

Deciding she may as well stretch her legs as opposed to sitting there staring into the dark, she carefully left the carriage, heading towards the lounge car. It was now about one o'clock in the morning and she wondered whether Gil might be there, might be waiting for her, hoping she'd changed her mind.

Anticipatory delight coursed through her as she drew nearer to the lounge car. Would he be there? She wasn't sure exactly what it was about Gil Fitzwilliam—*Professor* Gilbert Fitzwilliam—she mentally corrected herself— that had her in such a tizz.

Of course she appreciated his medical genius. She'd read all his papers and agreed with what he'd written. She'd marvelled at the research he'd undertaken and the medical breakthroughs he'd made to date. She was definitely attracted to his intellect but, then, what doctor wouldn't be? The man was incredible.

And incredibly good-looking too, a little voice said.

There was no point in denying—especially to herself—the way she felt when she was in Gil's presence. There was something about him, something that seemed to affect her in a way she'd never been affected before. Was it his looks or was it more than that? Perhaps it was the way he made her feel as though *she* were the genius.

Of course, she admitted to herself, the reason she'd been unable to sleep had nothing at all to do with the seats and everything to do with Gil. So here she was. Pushing open the door to the lounge car, eager and nervous at the same time to see whether or not he was around.

Walking through, ensuring the door closed firmly behind her, Phemie headed into the carriage, checking the first small recess where three ladies were all sitting and talking about their travel experiences. Two other people had their laptops plugged in and were busy staring at the screens.

Phemie moved on to the next recess, her mouth now completely dry, her heart pounding in triple time against her chest. Would he be there? If he was, what would she say to him? Oh. She hadn't thought this through. What if he thought she was chasing him? Stalking him? Her step faltered and she thought about turning back but forced herself to go on.

Two more steps and she was at the next recess, her gaze eagerly scanning the area and the four people sitting there. Her heart fell and her shoulders sagged.

None of them were Gil.

He wasn't there.

She was stupid.

It was the mantra which had been on constant replay through her head since she'd returned to her seat and forced herself to close her eyes and at least pretend to sleep. Professor Gilbert Fitzwilliam wasn't interested in her. In the social circles he mixed in she was way, way down at the bottom of the ladder. Just a girl he'd met on a train. That's all she was and she wished the silly, wistful side of her would recognise that fact.

It wasn't that she was after any sort of romantic relationship but she had to admit it had been nice to have a man look intently at her the way Gil had. He'd made her heart flutter, her stomach churn with anticipation and her knees go weak. That hadn't happened to her since high school when Danny Ellingham, the boy she'd had a secret crush on, had asked her to the school dance.

Of course, her parents had insisted she attend the dance, even though her mother's health hadn't been too good. It was one night, a few hours, she'd rationalised to herself as she'd dressed in the prettiest gown she'd been able to afford. What could possibly happen in a few hours?

A lot, it had turned out, although not where her parents and Anthony were concerned. They'd all made it through those hours yet for Phemie, that night had been one that had changed her life for ever.

Everything went according to plan. Danny picked her up from her home, chatted a few minutes with her father at the door. He was polite, he held her hand and proudly walked into the dance with his arm around her. She felt so happy and yet highly self-conscious. People were looking at the two of them, whispering about them, and some girls even had a hint of envy in their eyes. Danny was, after all, a good-looking guy. Joan Glastonbury, however, glared daggers at her. Phemie knew the other girl also liked Danny, but for tonight at least Danny had chosen *her*.

They danced, they talked and it seemed to be the night of her dreams. She'd liked Danny for a long time, sitting beside him in maths, being his lab partner in science, but she'd always thought he'd viewed her as nothing but a straight A student who could help him out from time to time. When he'd asked her to the dance, she'd been stunned but of course had said yes immediately. It wasn't until nearer the end of the night that she realised she knew very little about him.

Tommy Spitzner, the smartest boy in the school, had brought his cousin to the dance, a plump girl who had Down's syndrome.

'My parents made me bring her to the dance,' Tommy confessed when they had both been getting drinks. 'I don't mind. Lerleen's great and we get along fine.' Tommy laughed without humour. 'In fact, I think Lerleen's the one who brought me to the dance. My parents knew I didn't want to come but they keep telling me I'm too insular and said perhaps I should think of someone other than myself, etcetera, and now here I am at the stupid dance with my cousin.'

Both of them had looked over to where Lerleen was dancing by herself to the loud rock music. It was then that Phemie watched in horror as Danny and a few of his mates walked over to Lerleen and started teasing her. They pretended to ask her to dance then laughed and made rude comments when she eagerly accepted. Phemie's blood boiled over.

She'd marched over to Lerleen and stood next to the girl.

'Leave her alone.' She looked Danny square in the eyes, almost begging him to tell her it hadn't been his idea, that he'd been trying to stop the others, that he wasn't a part of it.

'We're just having a laugh,' Danny replied. 'It doesn't matter, Pheme. She doesn't go to this school and I don't think she even understands.'

'She may not, but I certainly do. Just because Lerleen has a disability doesn't make her any less of a person than you or I. She has feelings, she has rights and if you lot get excited by teasing and bullying people, especially ones who have a natural disposition to trust everyone they meet, then you're sadder than I thought.'

Tommy had come over and was guiding Lerleen away from the gathering crowd.

'You don't even know her,' Danny's friend pointed out.

'It doesn't matter. Picking on people is wrong and it most certainly isn't a means of fun, either.' She looked at Danny and shook her head. 'I can't believe you'd do something like this. You don't know what sort of damage you've caused that poor girl.'

'Why are you so defensive? Seriously, Phemie, how do you know what Tommy's half-wit cousin is feeling?'

'She's *not* a half-wit and I know what she's feeling because I understand Down's syndrome. My brother has it.'

'Down what?' one of the boys had asked.

She shook her head. 'We graduate in a few weeks from high school and you people have no idea about the world. You all live in your own little bubbles and don't care about anyone outside of them.'

'You have a brother like that girl?' Danny was almost aghast at the news. 'Why didn't I see him tonight? Are you ashamed of him? Hiding him away?'

'I'm not ashamed of him. He was in bed. He's younger than me and he goes to a different school.'

Danny then looked at his hands and wiped them on his jeans. 'I touched you. I held your hand. Eww. Did I catch it?'

'Nah, that only happens if you kissed her.' His mate sniggered.

Phemie shook her head in utter disgust. 'You

people make me sick.' A teacher came over then and
broken up the group. Phemie went to check on
Tommy and Lerleen, pleased to find the girl was OK.

'Thanks,' Tommy said. 'I think I'll take her
home now.'

Phemie nodded then turned to look at Danny, her
hopes and dreams crushed. The tingles he'd evoked
had turned to disgust but for a while there it had
been nice. Nice to feel as though someone liked her.

Now, though, she wasn't in high school, she
wasn't an adolescent and yet Gil had somehow
awakened those feelings, those sensations which
she'd thought totally dormant. Still, to have someone
of the opposite sex interested in her, to look at her
as though she were beautiful, to let her know she was
still mildly attractive was indeed exciting. The fact
he'd managed to evoke such a reaction made her
wonder if she *was* looking for something more than
she presently had—life in the outback, working with
good friends and spending her evenings alone.

Growing up, there had always been Anthony to
consider. Her parents had thought he would
always be living at home, that he'd never reach the
stage where he'd be capable of independent living.
Phemie had intended to stay close to home to
support her parents in any way she could.

Yet Anthony had surprised them all. Out of the two children in the Grainger family, he'd been the first one to move out of home into the assisted living facility where carers such as Liz were on hand to help them whenever required. He'd shown them all he was more than capable once his parameters had been set and now here he was, travelling across the country.

With Anthony not needing her as much, and her parents deciding this was their opportunity to travel overseas, Phemie had found herself floundering in a sea of confusion until an ex-colleague and friend from Royal Perth hospital, Dexter Crawford, had coaxed her to check out the RFDS.

It had been just what the doctor had ordered. Stepping outside her very comfortable comfort zone was something Phemie rarely did, mainly because she was needed in her comfort zone, needed by her parents and her brother, but with Anthony forging ahead on his own and her parents travelling, the RFDS had provided Phemie with the opportunity to do something for herself.

Granted, she was still helping people, as was her nature, and it hadn't taken her too long to settle down at the base where she'd been living for the past eight months. The staff she worked with, all of them, had been so extremely welcoming that she'd known she was in the right place.

Still, they were all married with families of their own and at times she felt the odd one out—the single one—which made her feel more isolated then the vast landscape of the outback.

Would it be so bad to have Gil come back to the base with her? It would only be for a week—seven days—and then he'd be gone. They'd experienced an instant connection—or, at least, she had. There was a good chance she was way off target but, still, having him around, knowing he could never stay…it might make her feel a little more normal for a while. She admired him as a professional and there was no denying she could certainly learn a lot from him in a professional capacity.

Just the thought of having him at the base made her skin prickle with anticipatory delight and her heart rate started to increase. No. She damped down those emotions. Attraction or not, she wasn't looking for a relationship.

'Phemie. I'm awake. Are you?'

A smile spread across her lips as she pushed her thoughts back into the box marked 'Do Not

OPEN' and opened her eyes to look at her brother.
'I'm awake.'

'I'm really excited. I get to go to *Sydney*.'

He made it sound as though he'd travelled to the
moon and just for a split second she wished she
could see the world as Anthony did—a place of
wonder and enjoyment simply waiting to be
explored. 'I know, love.' She placed a hand on his
cheek. 'How about you go and get changed out of
your pyjamas and we'll head to the dining car so
you can have something to eat.'

Childlike delight lit his features as he talked excitedly about what was on his 'list' of things to do
today. He ticked them off on his fingers and
Phemie listened patiently. It was part of Anthony.
He needed to get everything sorted out clearly in
his mind before he did anything

Phemie spent the rest of the morning helping Liz
and passing the time until the train pulled into
Sydney's central railway station. She didn't see Gil
in the dining car or the lounge carriage or anywhere
else for that matter and after they'd disembarked
from the train and had collected their luggage,
Phemie said goodbye to Anthony and his friends.

'Stay safe. Remember to only cross the road at

traffic lights. Don't go out at night time. Listen to Liz. And call me. Every night.'

'To say goodnight to Phemie.' Anthony nodded, content to accept her instructions.

'Exactly.' She hugged him close. 'I love you.'

'I love you, Phemie,' he responded, and squeezed her tight just as a child would.

She watched him get onto the minibus that would take them to their lodgings, with promises from Liz that she'd make sure Anthony called every day. Phemie waved goodbye, blowing kisses until the minibus was out of sight.

Sighing, she looked around, bringing her thoughts back to her own life and the next obstacle that lay before her. She needed to hail a taxi and get to the conference hotel. There were no scheduled events until tomorrow morning's welcome breakfast, which was held for the presenters, the conference not really starting until Monday. Still, she was looking forward to having a proper shower, as opposed to the one she'd had on the train, swaying to and fro with a few drops of water landing on her skin, and hopefully managing to catch up on her sleep.

Looking up and down the street, she realised there wasn't a vacant taxi in sight. All the other train passengers had taken them whilst she'd been fussing over her brother. She pulled out her mobile phone and was about to punch in the number for the taxi service when a black car pulled to the kerb beside her. She was about to pick up her luggage and move to another spot when the rear passenger window slid smoothly down.

'May I be so bold as to offer you a lift?' The deep, accented tone she'd dreamt about washed over her.

Phemie glanced up from her phone to look directly into the brown, hypnotic eyes of the man she'd been hard-pressed to stop thinking about ever since they'd first met.

'Gil.'

He stepped from the car as the chauffeur came round and started to put Phemie's luggage in the boot. 'I'm presuming you're on your way to the conference hotel?'

'Yes.' She looked into his gorgeous face and tried not to sigh. He was so incredibly good-looking. There were no two ways about it.

'Then you must allow me to give you a lift.' He held the rear passenger door for her and as her luggage had already been stowed in the boot, she really had no option but to accept.

'Uh…thank you,' she replied as she climbed into the back seat.

'Hello, there.'

Phemie was momentarily startled at the other person sitting in the back of the car. She sat next to him and then found herself sandwiched between the two men as Gil climbed in beside her. Whilst there was more than enough room for the three of them, she was incredibly self-conscious of the warmth radiating from the professor.

'Euphemia Grainger, meet William Hartnell.'

'Pleased to meet you, Dr Grainger.' William shook her hand politely.

'William is my personal aide and right-hand man,' Gil explained.

'And his left hand too, sometimes. I also double as the gopher and bodyguard.' William leaned a little closer and said in a stage whisper, 'I'd even take a bullet for him.'

Phemie turned to look at Gil in horror and concern. 'You have people shooting at you?'

Gil laughed. 'No. William was merely joking. I apologise for his warped sense of humour. I guess as we've been travelling together for almost a year now, we're too used to each other's ways.'

'OK.' Phemie decided to simply clasp her hands in her lap and sit nice and still until the car arrived at the hotel. She needed to concentrate, to keep her mind firmly under control and not allow the sensation of being this close to Gil to affect her. Of course, they'd been much closer, given that she'd fallen on him when the train had made its emergency stop, but that touch had been accidental. She was also trying to fight the way his scent was winding itself around her, the warmth of his body radiating out to encompass her. She prayed for green lights all the way to the hotel because the sooner she could put a bit of distance between herself and Gil, the sooner she'd be able to start thinking coherently again.

'I take it Anthony's safely away?'

'Yes. Uh…thank you for asking.'

'When does the group fly back to Perth?'

'Wednesday.' The conversation felt stilted but she tried not to worry about it. Gil was the one who'd offered her the lift so as far as she was concerned he could make all the effort at conversation. Besides, she was too busy keeping her equilibrium under strict control.

'And when will *we* be leaving Sydney?'

'Sorry?' William chimed in before Phemie could answer. '*We*? What do you mean? Has something extra been added to your schedule?'

Gil shook his head. 'After this conference ends,

I officially have one week's leave to do with as I see fit. Phemie, here, works for the Royal Flying Doctor Service. I'm going to spend a week in the outback with her.'

'You want to go to the outback instead of the beach?'

'Correct.'

'The rest of the team don't have to—?'

'No. You all have the right to choose what it is you want to do for that last week.'

'And you want to go to the outback?' William looked at Gil as though he'd grown an extra head.

Phemie felt as though she were at a ping-pong match. The two men were clearly friends but it was also clear that William didn't like being kept out of the loop, especially when it pertained to his boss.

She looked straight ahead. *Green lights. Please?*

'Phemie's going to try and pull some strings to see if I can return to the RFDS base with her instead of heading up to see the tropical coast.'

William pursed his lips for a moment before opening the folder that was on his lap. He took out a pen and made a notation. 'Dr Grainger, I'll be needing your cellphone number and a contact for the RFDS base.'

Phemie turned and looked at William, shaking her head in confusion. 'No. Um…this is all a bit premature. I haven't even spoken to my boss yet. Nothing is set in stone.' She was really starting to feel pressured and she didn't like it one bit. She liked things neat and organised and all hospital corners. Not higgledy-piggledy like this. If Gil wanted to come and see where she worked, she would talk to her boss but she wasn't going to be pushed around, having people making her life miserable.

'Which is why I need your contact details. So we can liaise and iron out travel plans,' William pointed out, pen poised.

Phemie looked at Gil and he could see she wasn't going to play ball—at least not William's way.

'Back off for the moment, William,' he remarked.

'Gil.' Phemie spoke clearly. 'I'll speak to my boss tonight and see what I can do. I need to find out if you can legally come and help but there will be a lot of red tape to get through. As I've already mentioned, I'm not sure I can promise anything. I'll let you know—both of you.' She turned to look at William, making sure he knew he wasn't being kept out of any loop. 'As soon as I have news. But until then this topic is off limits. I have to present a paper at the conference on Monday and I don't need any other interruptions. Understood?'

Gil could see the strain on her face and nodded. 'Understood, Phemie.'

She relaxed a little and was pleased when the car slowed down, hoping they'd finally arrived at the hotel. When she looked out the front windscreen it was to discover they were standing still in the middle of traffic. So much for green lights all the way.

'Problem?' Gil asked the chauffeur.

'Not sure, sir. Just a moment, I'll check to see if I can find out what the problem might be.'

'I hope it's not an accident,' William murmured as the chauffeur made a phone call. 'We're delayed enough as it is.'

'Sydney always has traffic jams.' Phemie tried not to shift around in her seat. She couldn't see much out the front window and moving to try and catch a glimpse of what might indeed be holding them up was only causing her to brush up even more against Gil.

'Good heavens,' Gil muttered, then, before she was aware of what he was doing, he'd unbuckled his seat belt and was opening his door.'

'Gil?' she called.

'What are you—? No don't,' William protested.

'Stay in the car. Gilbert?' But it was no use. The professor had disappeared. The chauffeur in the front seat was still making calls, trying to discover the reason for the delay.

'He's always like this,' William complained, and pulled his own phone from his pocket, pressing a button on his speed dial. A moment later he too was talking on his phone and Phemie wished on all the sanity she could muster that she'd had the presence of mind to decline Gil's offer of a lift and to find her own way of getting to the conference hotel. Even if it had meant she'd right now be sitting on board a bus stuck in the same traffic jam, at least she wouldn't have to be putting up with the prima donnas around her.

When the rear passenger door was wrenched open, she almost jumped out of her skin.

'Accident. Two cars, at least, from what I could see. It didn't happen that long ago. Emergency services have been called but we need to act now. Out.'

Phemie didn't need to be told twice and after he'd ordered the chauffeur to pop the car boot, Gil retrieved a small medical kit. 'It's all I've got.'

'It'll have to do. We can improvise wherever

possible.' They started walking away from his town car, both of them ignoring William's protests.

'Improvise, eh?'

'Sure.' She grinned at him. 'If you want to survive a week in the outback, Professor, you'd best be a fast learner.'

A spark of interested delight flashed into his eyes, which left Phemie catching her breath with a wave of tingling anticipation. 'Oh, I am, Dr Grainger. Just you wait and see how fast I can learn.'

CHAPTER FIVE

As THEY walked past the parked cars, some impatiently honking their horns, others deciding to switch off their engines, Phemie was glad the accident hadn't happened in one of the tunnels. Thankfully, from what she could remember of Sydney, they weren't too far from Sydney General hospital, which meant that help would be on its way sooner rather than later. All she and Gil really needed to do was provide triage for the patients and provide whatever care they could.

'I thought there were only two cars involved.' Gil pointed to where there were two other cars, having slammed on their brakes and skidded into other cars.

'It looks like a backwards letter K,' Phemie remarked. There were three lanes of traffic, all of them now blocked by cars strewn across the lanes. Some of them had stopped perilously close to each other but had managed to avoid crashing. Of the others, they could see that some had only been hit in front, others were crumpled at both ends but the main car, right in the centre of the crush, appeared bashed from all sides.

'How do you want to play this?' Phemie asked, more than happy to defer to Gil.

'Take a look at the passengers in the surrounding cars. I'll check the main one to see whether there are any survivors.' There were two men out of their cars who were also trying to help and Gil walked up to them.

'My colleague and I are doctors. Have you any information on the situation?'

'Uh…we've called for emergency services—'

'I did that,' the younger man interjected, and Phemie realised he could be no more than twenty years old.

'Good thinking,' she praised. 'What's your name?'

'Connor. That's my dad, Jim.'

'I did twenty years in the army,' Jim remarked.

'Then you'll be able to keep a clear head.' Gil nodded. 'If you can keep traffic controlled and maybe find a way to clear a drivable path through for the emergency crews, that would be of great assistance. Take point where needed.'

'Yes, Doctor,' Jim replied, almost snapping a salute.

Gil turned to Phemie. 'Go check out those cars.' He pointed to the ones at the rear of the mess. 'Report back as soon as you can. I'll do the same.'

With that he headed off to the car in the centre as Jim and his son started taking control of the traffic. Phemie walked over to the end car and peered inside. Only one person.

'Hi. I'm Phemie. I'm a doctor. I'm here to help.' She'd said those words, or a variation of them, time and time again. It was true, too. She'd become a doctor so she could help people, patch them up and support them in their time of need.

This poor man required her attention now and she soon realised he was having difficulty remembering his name. After a brief examination, she could see a large bump already forming on his head. She needed him to keep as still as possible until the ambulance arrived. Phemie looked around his car in the hope that she could find something to keep his head supported.

She found a newspaper and a towel amongst his belongings in the back seat and was able to fashion a neck brace. All the while she worked, she continued talking to him, asking him questions,

getting him to say the alphabet and count to
twenty—anything to stop him from resting too
much and falling asleep. Keeping his mind active
was very important if he'd suffered a brain injury.

Carefully, she came from behind him and
managed to manoeuvre the makeshift neck brace
into place with little fuss. 'There. That should help
but you must stay as still as possible,' she instructed. She looked around them outside and
realised a few more people had left their cars and
were wanting to help out.

She climbed from the car and called to a woman
who was standing not too far away. 'Hi. What's
your name?' Phemie asked.

'Nora.'

'Great. Nora, can you come and talk to this man?
He's sustained a head injury and I need him to keep
still but not to go to sleep.'

'OK. What's his name?'

'He can't remember at the moment. That's not
important. Just ask him to say his times tables or
count or spell words, things like that.'

'OK. I can do that.'

'Good.' Phemie took a deep breath, then headed
towards the next car. Gil was striding purpose-
fully towards her.

'How are you doing?'

She pointed. 'Patient in this car has an elevated pulse, sluggish pupils and a bad bump to the head. I've fashioned a neck brace to keep him stable and have a lady talking to him to keep him lucid.'

'You fashioned a neck brace?' Gil took a few steps closer and peered into the car, then turned back to Phemie and shook his head in wonderment. 'Good improvising.'

'Thank you. What's next?'

'Ground zero car is a mess. Both front passengers are dead. I think, but I'm not entirely sure, that there may be another person in the back of the car. Even if I'm right, it's all so mangled, I'm presuming they would have died on impact.'

Phemie shook her head and crossed her arms over her chest. 'Any idea what may have caused the accident?'

'I'm too busy right now to figure out the whys and wherefores. Let's just help as many people as we can.'

As they headed off to check on other vehicles, they both stopped for a moment when they heard the sounds of sirens heading in their direction.

'A welcome sound,' Gil murmured.

It wasn't long before they received help, the

paramedics attending to Phemie's head injury patient and fire crews sorting through the wreckage. The police took over from Jim and his son, thanking them for their assistance, and soon a very slow parade of cars passed by as they continued to work.

Two women, both in their thirties, had escaped unharmed except for seat-belt bruises. 'We still need you to go to the hospital to be evaluated,' Phemie said firmly to one of the women who was eager just to go home and lie down. 'Sometimes, in situations such as this, your body can be in shock and other symptoms can present themselves a few hours after the initial accident. Please,' she urged. 'Go to the hospital, let them monitor you for the next few hours. It's a necessary precaution.'

'Dr Grainger is absolutely right.' Gil spoke from behind her, pulling off a pair of gloves. At the sound of his soothing English accent, Phemie felt a mass of tension leave her body. How was it he could have such a calming effect on her? Perhaps keeping him around at the Didja base for a week wasn't such a bad idea after all. They could do clinics, assist with house calls and emergencies then at the end of the day they could sit out on the verandah. Gil could talk to her in his normal easy-flowing tones and her body would instantly unwind. So rich, so deep, so…Gil.

'Wouldn't you agree, Dr Grainger?'

It was then Phemie realised she was standing there, staring up at him as though he'd just hung the moon. She gave herself a mental shake and nodded. 'Absolutely, Professor.' She honestly had no idea what she was agreeing to but if Gil had said it, it must be correct, right? When she turned to look back at the two women, Phemie realised that they, too, appeared to be under Gil's thrall.

Both women were looking at him as though he was the most perfect male specimen they'd ever come across and they would be more than willing to do as he'd suggested on the proviso that *he* was the doctor who looked after them during their time of investigation.

'You're a professor?' The first woman preened. 'English, handsome and a professor.'

'Are you married?' the second woman asked, fluttering her eyelashes at him.

Whilst Phemie thought the question gauche and impolite, it was only then that she realised that even *she* didn't know the answer to that question. All this time she'd been looking at him, mildly flirting with him, enjoying his company—as he had obviously been enjoying hers, given that a few times she'd been positive he'd wanted to kiss her—and yet she hadn't even considered the possibility that he might be married. It was so unlike her not to be sure. She planned everything. She was Miss Hospital Corners!

Even more surprisingly, she realised she was holding her breath, along with the other two women, as they waited for his answer.

'No,' he replied politely, but the firmness in his tone indicated there was a lot more to what he was not saying. His back had become more rigid, his shoulders were firmly squared and he was clenching the used gloves tightly in his hands. It was as though he was channelling all his frustration, his annoyance, his pain into the gloves in order to keep himself under control.

Pain? Gil glanced at Phemie and, yes, there it was. A deep, unabated pain in his eyes, and it only confirmed her feeling that there was a lot more going on. What had happened to him? Had he lost a loved one? Had some tragedy struck his life? Perhaps he had been married and it had ended in divorce? A bad marriage wasn't something anyone liked to talk about with random strangers. Was Gil's life in turmoil? Could that possibly be one of the reasons why he'd embarked on the travelling fellowship? Was he running away from his life?

'Let's get you ladies over to the ambulance.' Gil turned and called for one of the police officers to come and escort the women to the paramedics. 'Phemie,' Gil said when they were alone again, 'I was just talking to Kirk, the lead fireman, and he said there *is* someone in the back of the centre car.'

'Oh, no.' Phemie had looked at the wreckage and hadn't been able to see anyone but, then, the rear of the car had been so bent and pushed out of shape, it had been impossible to see everything.

'They have specialised equipment to pick up heat signatures, which tells them how many bodies—that sort of thing. They found a heat signature in the back.'

'Wait, but that would mean—'

'The person's still alive.'

'Oh, my gosh. All this time. If we'd known…' Compassionate pain filled her eyes and Gil marvelled at the woman before him. She'd handled herself so professional, so brilliantly with the emergency and even though he knew that working with the RFDS, she'd often be called to assist in all kinds of different and unique situations, to see her actually working her way methodically through what was required filled him with pride. It was an odd sensation, feeling proud of this woman he barely knew, but each different facet of her personality she allowed him to see only enhanced the gravitational pull he felt towards her.

'Is there anything we can do to help with the extraction?' Phemie started walking towards the centre car.

'Better leave it to the fire crews. They have the equipment to cut the person out. They've already peeled back the roof, which gives them better access.'

'To the people in the front,' she pointed out. 'But the rear of the car is so mangled it's going to take them a lot longer to get to that person. It might end up being too late.' Phemie stood back from the centre car, watching the emergency services team do their jobs.

They were in the process of shifting the two deceased bodies from the front of the car, hoping it would give them better access to the rear. The ground had already been sprayed with foam to ensure no leaking fuel ignited. This, however, made the area quite slippery, especially as she was only wearing a pair of flat boots beneath her jeans. Her light green shirt was covered by her navy jumper and Phemie was glad she'd dressed comfortably that morning. Then again, she'd anticipated already being at her hotel by now where she would have showered and changed into clothes more befitting a medical presenter at the conference.

Gil was dressed in a suit and had discarded his jacket before they'd left the car, his tie was now missing and she wondered whether he'd used it as an improvised tourniquet or whether it was rolled up in his trouser pocket. His crisp chambray shirt was no longer crisp, but was streaked with grime, blood and dirt.

It didn't matter. What they wore, how they looked, it didn't matter. What mattered was the trapped person and as Phemie looked on, she wondered if there wasn't a way to extract the patient from the rear of the car rather than going through the front.

'The only place that person could be is lying on the back seat floor of that car.' Phemie spoke clearly.

With the way the car seemed to have folded in on itself, she had a point. 'That's not a lot of room.'

'A child?'

'A teenager? I think we can safely surmise it's not a six-foot man.'

'Agreed. He simply wouldn't fit into such a tiny space. A woman?'

'That's more likely, but how did they get to the floor? With her seat belt on, it would have been an impossibility.'

'Maybe the seat belt snapped. Maybe they unbuckled it just for an instant to pick something up off the floor.'

'Too many scenarios and no need to puzzle our way through them. What we need to focus on is the best way to extract the person.'

'Or at least to get medical aid to them so that whilst the extraction process continues, they're at least getting analgesia and fluids.'

'If it was possible to…' He stopped and thought some more, trying to study the mess before them.

'Cut through the rear? That's what I was thinking but then the petrol tank poses a problem.'

'What about going in—?' Gil broke off and growled with impatience. 'The only way is what the crews are doing now. Removing the front passengers so we can get to the person in the back.'

'Frustrating.'

'I don't usually attend accident sites,' Gil murmured. 'Not in the last few years at any rate.'

'Prefer to stay in the hospital and wait for the patients to be brought to you?'

'Something like that.' Gil frowned at the slow,

meticulous way the emergency crews were doing their best to get to the trapped person. It made him think about the plane accident that had taken the life of his wife and baby daughter. Had she panicked as the plane had plummeted? Had she felt any pain? Had she felt alone? Had she been thinking of him?

Gil hadn't thought about his wife's death in this much detail since the funeral. After he'd buried his family, he'd walked away, determined not to look back, determined to lock his heart up and never open himself up for so much pain ever again. He'd thrown himself into his work, wanting to make a difference with his research, with his developments. He'd lost weight, was hardly sleeping and, as William had termed it, was 'becoming a shadow of his former self'.

The travelling fellowship had seemed like a good idea. He could step outside his comfort zone whilst still remaining firmly in it. When you travelled, when you met new people every week, when you spoke in lecture theatre after lecture theatre on similar topics, you could still feel very alone.

That's what had happened to him. It was why he'd initially been looking forward to ending the tour and going back to London, even if it was only to attempt to have some sort of normal life. That was before he'd met the enchanting Euphemia Grainger.

She'd made him feel alive as he hadn't felt in years. She'd made him think about personal issues he'd wanted to leave boxed up in the far recesses of his mind. She'd made him realise he was become more attracted to her the more time they spent together.

Watching her now, watching the way she was empathising with their unknown patient, how she was as eager as he was to get in there and provide whatever medical care they could, it reminded him of himself. He had a need to be there for people, to give help, to solve problems. It appeared Phemie was cut from the same cloth.

'Dr Grainger, is it?' One of the firemen walked over to where she and Gil were standing, watching silently.

'Phemie, meet Kirk.' Gil quickly introduced them.

'Phemie, we need someone short enough to slide into the car and assess the patient as best you can. All of us…' Kirk indicated the police and fire staff '…are too tall.'

'Wait.' Gil held up his hand. 'You want Phemie to do what?' He wasn't sure he liked what he was hearing. All his English sensibilities started to bristle. Phemie was more than capable to doing what was asked, he had no doubt about that, but why her? So she was small. Surely there were other people who could do it. He would even volunteer to wedge himself into the small space but from Phemie's decisive look she was more than willing to do what was asked. His heart began to pound a concerned rhythm as he visualised her in that car.

'When we've finished clearing the front seats, we'll be needing someone, preferably with medical knowledge, to climb in and assess the patient. Dr Grainger seems the obvious choice. She's small enough and qualified.'

'That's fine.' Phemie nodded. 'How much room will I have?'

'You'll be able to get your arm through, possibly…' Kirk looked at Phemie's small hands. 'Both your hands.'

'Good. I'll go and talk to the paramedics and get set up.'

'Excellent.' Kirk headed back to his crew. As Phemie turned to head over to the ambulance, Gil reached out and stopped her.

'You can't climb into that car. It's not safe.' He left his hand on her arm, the warmth of his touch causing her body to flood with tingles.

'It's all right, Gil. It's not like I haven't done things like this before.'

'What?' His tone was incredulous. 'Are you completely insane? You're willingly and knowingly putting yourself in danger.' As he spoke the words, wanting desperately to change her mind, he also knew he had no right to ask, yet his protective urge towards her only seemed to be intensifying the more time they spent together.

It was insane. This wasn't like him at all. He knew Kirk had been right to ask Phemie. She had all the qualifications and she was small enough to fit into the space. He was also sure that if Kirk hadn't asked, Phemie would have volunteered. Still, the thought of Phemie climbing into that highly unstable vehicle made his stomach churn and his head whirl. But why?

'I'm helping someone in need and it's not *really* dangerous.' Why was he so concerned about this? He seemed almost adamant that she not be involved in this situation. Providing initial medical care was all well and good but when it turned serious, did Gil really expect her to pull back? 'I mean, I'm surrounded by emergency crew members who know what they're doing, the area has been doused with foam so there's little chance of the vehicle catching fire and, honestly, Gil, it's not the worst situation I've been in.'

Gil continued to hold her arm, not wanting to let her go. He took another step forward and then, to her surprise, placed his free hand on her cheek, caressing the soft skin there. Phemie froze, unable to move, unable to breathe, his soft, sweet touch creating havoc with her senses.

'I've seen how you work under pressure, Phemie. You're incredible. I'm not saying you're not capable of doing the work, just that...' He exhaled slowly and swallowed, his Adam's apple working up and down his magnificent throat. 'Be careful. Please. For me. Take extra care.'

Phemie was slightly puzzled at his soft, tender words, not sure why someone she hardly knew that well was so concerned for her well-being. Perhaps it was because he knew how much she was needed, especially after he'd met Anthony. Yes. That had to be it. Gil was merely showing this much concern because he was worried about Anthony. It was the only explanation she could come up with.

'I promise,' she remarked and tried not to nestle her cheek further into his palm. To feel him touching her like that, to be the recipient of such a caress, it made her mind jump all over the place and the last thing she needed right now was to lose her focus.

With strength she hadn't known she possessed, Phemie forced herself to step back, breaking all contact between them. Resolutely she squared her shoulders and lifted her chin. 'I need to focus.'

'Of course.' Gil also took a step back instantly berating himself for having shown her how much he'd come to care for her in such a short time. 'Do what you need to do.'

With a brief nod, Phemie walked over to the ambulance, trying to push the memory of his touch into the far recesses of her mind. Gil had touched her before, he'd held her firmly in his arms and been so close, they could easily have kissed. This time, though, his concern had been more personal rather than simply physical. It was dangerous.

CHAPTER SIX

GIL watched as Phemie was helped into the front passenger section of the car the fire crews had cleared. She crammed herself into place and was able to reach through a small gap to insert an IV line and check on the patient.

As she'd finished, the patient started to stir and Phemie managed to ascertain the woman's name was Mary and that she was twenty-one. Gil handed Phemie a syringe of analgesics, which she administered intravenously.

Apart from that, there wasn't much for Phemie to do except to stay in her cramped position whilst the crews continued their methodical removal of metal. Every ten minutes Phemie would listen to Mary's chest, managing to fit the stethoscope through the opening and then twisting around so her arm was almost fully extended in order to reach properly.

Gil was able to keep a close watch on the IV

line, which was hanging on a makeshift rig above Phemie.

'How does it sound?' Mary asked, as Phemie carefully drew her arm back from listening to the heart.

'Like a heart should sound,' Phemie replied, a smile in her voice as she unhooked the instrument from her ears. 'So, you said you have a brother? Older or younger?' It was important for her to talk to Mary, to keep her as calm as possible whilst the extraction team worked all around her.

'Younger. He's only just turned thirteen.'

'Eight years. That's quite a gap. Any other siblings?'

'No. My parents had a lot of trouble conceiving. My mum was forty-two when she had Daniel.'

Phemie's neck began to prickle. 'That's rather late.' She hedged carefully, knowing full well that women who had babies later in life were more likely to have children with birth defects. 'Were there any problems with the baby? I mean, your brother is he…?' She paused, trying to think of a diplomatic way to ask without upsetting Mary.

'Daniel's gorgeous. Then again, I'm a little biased, although when people first meet him, they're a bit shocked to find he has Down's syndrome. I just don't see it any more. He's just…Daniel.'

Phemie nodded, even though Mary couldn't see her. It was what she'd been expecting Mary to say and in that moment she felt an instant connection with her patient. They were both older sisters to younger brothers with Down's. Mary would know exactly how Phemie felt about things without the need to explain or expand. The frustration, the guilt, the utter devotion. 'My brother has Down's, too,' she confessed.

'Really?' Mary sounded almost excited. 'Isn't that a strange coincidence. What's his name?'

'Anthony. He's four years younger than me.'

'So he's a grown up?'

'He is.'

'That's fantastic. What's he like?'

Phemie smiled as she talked of Anthony, pleased she'd found a topic that would keep her patient's mind occupied.

'I've often wondered what the future will hold for Daniel. Some people can be cruel and he's just so friendly to everyone he meets.'

Didn't she know that all too well. 'It's part of their nature,' Phemie murmured, thinking of all the times she and her parents had tried to instil the lesson of 'stranger danger' into Anthony. 'I think people are often afraid of what they don't understand.'

'They let their own ignorance blind them.'

'Exactly.' Phemie shook her head and smiled. 'It's so nice to talk to someone who really understands.'

'Me too.' There was a smile in Mary's voice. 'I used to love helping my mother look after him when he was little, and now that he's a teenager I guess I still worry about him. I love taking him out, going to the movies or out for pizza—that's his favourite food. We're really good friends even though there's such a huge age difference.'

'Friends?' Phemie was filled with envy. From the way Mary was talking, it was clear she'd had a *sibling* relationship with her brother, rather than being another carer, and that close brother-sister thing was what Phemie had always wanted.

'Sure. I guess I was so happy to finally have a baby brother that I've been a little possessive of him.'

'You spend a lot of time with him?' Phemie closed her eyes, not only feeling sick because she wasn't one hundred per cent sure Mary would be able to spend much time with him in the future but also feeling guilty that she'd never voluntarily spent time with Anthony. The times she'd taken him out had all been because she'd felt obliged to help her parents. Even though there was a bigger age difference between Mary and her brother than between herself and Anthony, it was the feelings in the heart that mattered most.

'I do. Or I did.' Mary's voice dropped to a whisper and she became silent.

'Mary?' No answer. Phemie looked up, checked the drip, glanced at Gil, who was standing by ready to give her anything she needed. She'd forgotten he was there, listening to her conversation. It didn't matter, though. Not now. Only Mary mattered. 'Mary?' She tried again, her tone a little more forceful. 'Mary, tell me what Daniel's favourite movie is. Anthony likes superhero movies. Mary?'

Phemie heard the sound of the other woman sniffing, as though she was quietly crying. 'Uh…he likes superheroes too. Don't most boys?'

She breathed a sigh of relief at Mary's reply. 'I guess they do.'

'My favourite is the one about the ice-skating princess. I even took up ice-skating because of that movie, wanting to glide and spin as gracefully as she does.'

'And can you?'

'I can. I don't skate in competitions or anything but it's where I go when I want to relax or when things aren't going right.' There was a pause. 'I keep imagining that's where I am right now.

Skating around the rink, the breeze on my face, my arms out behind me as all the problems slide off and float away, leaving me free.'

A lump formed in Phemie's throat at Mary's words and she looked up at Gil. There was no need for either of them to say anything. Gil's gaze confirmed that he'd heard Mary and the look in Phemie's eyes said she wanted to find a place like that for herself, a place where all her stresses and worries could slide off and float away on the breeze. Gil's brown eyes encompassed her, making her feel safe and secure, letting her hope the place she might find that release was within his arms.

'Every year at Christmas,' Mary continued, 'my mum and I sit down and watch it together. It's like our tradition. I want to do that with my daughter. Or I did.' She fell silent for a moment and then Phemie could hear the sounds of crying again. When Mary spoke, it was with quiet acceptance. 'I'm not going to make it, am I?' It may have been spoken as a rhetorical question but Phemie decided to answer it.

'You have a very solid crew of workers who would beg to differ. I know it's hard to wait but everyone's doing everything they can. We're working as a team and we're going to get you out.' She was adamant about that.

'I'm scared, Phemie.'

'I know.' Phemie leaned forward, contorted herself through the wreckage again and found Mary's hand, holding it as reassuringly as she could. 'I know.' Her own tears slid down her cheeks and she closed her eyes, knowing she needed to be strong for Mary. They were getting closer to extraction with each passing minute. 'Um…' She sniffed and quickly schooled her voice to portray a confidence she didn't feel. 'What other types of sport do you like?'

Phemie successfully managed to distract Mary while Gil stood in silence, watching the strength that flowed through her. She was quite a woman.

The entire time Phemie was in the vehicle, his body was taut, his mind focused. It was as though he was on red-alert, watching carefully, working through differing scenarios just in case things went haywire. Phemie was putting herself in harm's way and whilst he understood her need to be helpful, he didn't like it.

Apart from that last searing look, she'd kept her focus on Mary, as it should be. Yet Gil had also noticed the way she'd not only physically but mentally removed herself from his touch when he'd caressed her cheek. Was she upset with him?

Had he crossed a line? Had he gone too far, too fast? The fact that he had no idea why she affected him the way she did was a constant puzzle yet his need to feel that soft, sweet skin had been too powerful for him to resist.

Even if he did accept there was something of a more personal nature developing between them, the main question remained—what on earth could he do about it? He would be leaving her country within a very short period of time and returning to his own world of rules, regulations and red tape. Now, though, he wasn't sure he wanted to go. Was that why he was latching onto Phemie? She was like a breath of fresh air, one that had blown right into his neatly ordered life and completely disrupted it. Had he become so closed off, so insular that a beautiful and intelligent woman like Euphemia Grainger could just waltz in and shake him up? Maybe so.

After June and Caitie had died, Gil had locked himself into a world of work. He hadn't been able to help his wife and his baby girl but that hadn't meant there weren't other people who needed him. So he'd worked, he'd researched, he'd developed different means and methods for procedures and then he'd toured the world, telling all who would listen, hoping to make a difference somewhere, some place, some time.

However, had his self-enforced prison meant he'd completely lost touch with the real world— the world of beautiful and intelligent women? Sure, he had female colleagues and he respected them but never had one attract him the way Phemie did. He'd been more than content to remain alone, to remain in his own little world…until he'd met her.

Did he have to stay alone? Was there…could there be some possibility that his life *hadn't* ended when his family had been cruelly taken from him? It was a thought he'd never considered and he filed it away to take out later when he was in a less intense atmosphere.

The fire crews had made some progress but now they were getting to the stage that if they moved too much too soon, it could do more damage to Mary's already traumatised body.

'We're going to need to stabilise her as best we can before we move this last section,' Kirk was explaining. 'Unfortunately, we can't get the pat-slide in, the portable stretcher is too bulky so we're not exactly sure how best to keep Mary still while we continue to cut her out.'

Kirk was mainly talking to Gil as the two men surveyed the situation. From Phemie's vantage point she could see exactly what they were talking about. She'd just finished checking Mary's vitals.

'Are there some spare sheets or blankets in the ambulance?' she asked.

'I presume so,' Kirk answered,

'And rope? Do you have some rope?'

'Plenty of rope.' Kirk nodded.

'Then why not use the blanket and rope to fashion a sling? If Gil can manage to slide in around the side where you've already removed that back section and feed it through, hopefully I'll be able to reach in and pull it up this side of Mary, thereby—'

'Keeping her suspended in a sling whilst we lift the rest of the wreckage off her.' Kirk finished her sentence, nodding with excitement before racing off to get things organised.

'You really do think outside the box, don't you?' Gil remarked.

'Improvisation is a big part of outback medicine. You'll see that.' Phemie looked at him, the midday sun shining down on them. Thank goodness it was autumn rather than the height of summer otherwise they'd all be cooking in the Aussie heat and humidity by now. As she looked at Gil, the way the sun's rays were surrounding him almost gave him a sort of halo effect. It only served to enhance his good looks, his dark hair, his hypnotic eyes, his square chiselled jaw.

Phemie forced herself to look away. Staring at him wasn't the right way to keep herself under control. He was a colleague, possibly a friend. Nothing more. She started talking to Mary again, keeping the woman as alert as possible, given the circumstances. The last blood-pressure reading had shown they were currently replacing the fluids almost as fast as Mary was losing them. It wasn't a good sign. The internal or external bleeding— or both, depending on what they eventually found—needed to be stopped as soon as possible and once more Phemie experienced a high level of impatience, even though she knew everyone on the crew was doing everything they could as fast as they possibly could.

The paramedics had already called through to Sydney General and alerted A and E to the situation, giving as much of a breakdown of Mary's injuries as Phemie could presently ascertain. Things didn't look good but she wasn't going to let that deter her and pushed the negative thoughts to the back of her mind. She needed to keep talking to Mary, doing all she could to take the woman's mind off what was currently happening to her.

'Anthony loves tactile things,' she was telling Mary, the conversation having returned to the topic of their brothers. 'When he was younger, every time we walked into a new room, he'd have to touch the floor with his hand to feel the difference in the surface.'

'That's what Daniel does, too.'

'My mother, who is a total germaphobe, would carry around little wash cloths to wipe him down every time he'd run his hands all over the floor.' Phemie smiled at the memory. 'It doesn't seem so long ago and now, he's off travelling around Sydney somewhere with his friends.' She hoped to goodness he hadn't been caught in this traffic jam and made a mental note to call him when she arrived at the hotel.

'Really? He's travelling? He is so brave.'

'That's Anthony. Last year, he even moved away from home.'

'Now I know you're kidding.'

'Not in the slightest. He now resides in an independent living facility, specifically designed for adults with Down's, and he loves it.'

'It's so great to hear you talk like this, for me to

know that Daniel's future isn't going to be so restricted by society.'

'On the contrary. I confess, I get a little jealous of him.'

'I know what you mean. Sometimes I wish I had Daniel's outlook on life. He's always so positive.'

Gil listened as he worked with the crews, pleased he had the opportunity to learn more about Phemie. He was highly intrigued by her and knowing more gave him a stronger feeling of control. Losing loved ones, especially his gorgeous baby girl, had left him more determined to control everything as closely as he could.

They all worked together and finally the makeshift sling was in place. Gil was ready with a neck brace to slip it around Mary's neck the instant he had access to her. Phemie had given Mary another dose of painkillers so her body wouldn't go into shock with what was about to happen. Having Mary lucid and able to follow instructions was going to be extremely helpful during the transfer process.

It would all happen quickly and everyone needed to be in position and on high alert. Phemie prepared Mary, talking her through what would happen so there were hopefully no surprises.

'I'm scared,' Mary said, and a lump lodged itself

in Phemie's throat as she reached out and took Mary's hand in hers.

'I know you are. You have every right to be scared but also know we're all here for you, to help you, to get you out. OK.'

'I know.'

Phemie could tell the young woman was crying and she didn't blame her. Tears welled in her own eyes and she quickly blinked them away. She needed to be ready, to be alert, to be completely focused.

'Ready?' Kirk asked Phemie.

'Ready.' She nodded. Gil, who was standing opposite Phemie, could see the struggle she'd just gone through and once again, as he watched her pull herself together, as she pushed away the personal and pulled on the professional, he marvelled at that inner strength she seemed to exude.

'On three,' Kirk announced. 'One, two, *three*.'

It all happened so fast—the wreckage being shifted, the fire and police members pulling on the ropes to elevate Mary and then Gil and the paramedics transferring Mary to the waiting ambulance stretcher.

'Phemie!' Mary called, and Phemie was helped out of the car and over to the waiting ambulance. She climbed inside and reached for Mary's hand.

'There. You're out. You're ready to go. You've been amazing,' Phemie encouraged.

'I want you to call my parents and tell them about Anthony. Let them know that Daniel's going to have a great life.'

Tears welled up in Phemie's eyes at Mary's words, their hands gripped tightly together. 'I'll call.' Even now, Mary was thinking of others and Phemie couldn't help but love this woman she barely knew. 'You are a remarkable woman, Mary. You're strong. Keep being strong.'

'Thank you.' Mary's words were soft and silent tears slid down her dirty, blood-stained cheeks. 'For being my lifeline.'

Too choked up to speak, Phemie smiled through her tears and then let go of Mary's hand and exited the ambulance. She had no jurisdiction here. She was just a doctor who had happened to be passing by when the accident had happened and had stopped to lend a hand. She had no authority at the hospital, she didn't know any of the surgeons who would operate on Mary, and the lack of control left her feeling bereft as the ambulance pulled away.

'Are you all right?' Gil asked from behind her, and it was then she became conscious of the warmth of his body.

'No.' The tears wouldn't go away. She couldn't control them and the instant Gil put a hand on her shoulder, Phemie turned and almost crumbled into his waiting arms, her tension being released through her heartfelt sobs.

No one chided her for letting her feelings come to the surface. No one seemed concerned that she'd let her emotions get the better of her. No one said anything as Gil simply held her whilst she cried. The crews continued with their work, cleaning up the debris so the entire three lanes could once more be open again to the thick city traffic.

Gil tightened his hold on her, wanting to keep her close, pleased he could be there for her when she needed him. Closing his eyes, he savoured the feel of her, the touch of her hair against his cheek, the way that even after everything she'd just been through, her subtle sunshine scent still managed to drive him to distraction.

'She's not going to make it. I know. I can tell,' she murmured against his chest, and tenderly Gil stroked her back.

'We did everything we could. Now it's up to the surgeons and Mary.'

Phemie pulled back, her tears starting to dry up as quickly as they'd come. 'I'm sorry,' she instantly apologised. So much for trying to keep her distance from Gil. Here she was, standing literally in the middle of the road in a strange city with the man's arms firmly around her. Looking up into his eyes, she wasn't sure what she expected to see. Would he be annoyed? The fact that his arms were still holding her should be evidence enough that he wasn't annoyed. Maybe he was embarrassed, not only for himself but for her as well. Some professional she was, blubbering over a patient. Had he held her close because he'd wanted to hide her embarrassment? Confusion ripped through her and was followed closely by self-consciousness.

She splayed her hands against his chest, getting ready to ease back, but when she finally looked into his gorgeous brown eyes she faltered, her fingers becoming sensitised to the firm male torso beneath his cotton shirt. Her breath caught in her throat as she continued to stare up at him just as he was staring down at her.

'We should probably think about heading off now,' Gil murmured, his Adam's apple working up and down as he swallowed. His voice was deep, personal and filled with repressed desire. It was strange. It was wrong but it was happening. Both of them knew it but neither wanted to accept it.

'Yes.' It was all the answer she was capable of giving because her mind was too busy controlling her need to stand on tiptoe to press her lips against his. The heat that suffused her at the thought did nothing to help with her resolve to keep her distance.

'We should, uh…'

'Go,' Phemie finished, and it was another second before both of them seemed to drop their hands in unison. They quickly said goodbye to Kirk, who shook hands with Gil but then surprised Phemie by enveloping her in a hug.

'Good work, Phemie. Nice to have met you. Might even come out to that outback place for a visit.'

Phemie smiled tiredly at him. 'Didja is a sight to behold, Kirk. You'd be more than welcome.'

Gil couldn't help the mild stirring of…was that jealousy? He pushed it aside but possessively put his arm around Phemie's waist and guided her away from the crews back to where William had had their chauffeur park the car out of the way. He didn't *do* jealousy.

When she was once more seated in the back of the car, Phemie leaned her head back on the soft head-rest and closed her eyes.

'Are you feeling all right?' Gil asked quietly.

'Tired.' She didn't open her eyes and was sort of

pleased when she felt his hand envelop her own. She knew she should have pulled away but the stress of being with Mary, of talking to her, of hearing Mary talk about her family and especially her brother…the whole situation was starting to catch up with her and Gil's support was more than welcome at the moment. She knew that once they arrived at the hotel, Gil would need to keep his distance. After all, he was the professor and, as such, needed to conduct himself in a highly professional manner. For now, though, she would take whatever he was offering.

Just this once, she wanted to imagine her life would turn out differently. She wanted to pretend that Gil was hers—the man of her dreams, just as she would be the woman of his. They would be heading to a conference together, as husband and wife. He would speak, give his views on various topics, and a few days later they'd return to the outback where their gaggle of three girls and two boys awaited them. Five, beautiful, healthy children.

The children would run around in the large open spaces surrounding the RFDS base whilst she and Gil sat on the verandah, sipping cool drinks as night-time fell. She would look at Gil and he would look at her, both of them with love in their hearts.

Phemie sighed with longing and let her mind continue to drift as Gil and William talked softly, their words blurring around her. She was surprised when Gil gently called her name, urging her to rouse, as they'd finally arrived at their hotel.

'What a journey,' William remarked as he checked a few things off on his folder. 'I thought we'd never get here.'

And now that they had, Phemie knew she had to let go of any sort of fantasy she might have entertained with regard to Gilbert Fitzwilliam. He was a stranger. Someone she'd met on a train. Someone who didn't factor into her plans for the future. Not now. Not ever.

'How are you feeling now?' he asked tenderly.

'Better.' Phemie smothered a yawn. 'I think I need to shower and change, though. No doubt that will improve the lethargy I'm currently experiencing.'

'And don't forget to give Anthony a call. He seems to live on pure energy. Maybe he can transmit some down the phone line.'

Phemie smiled tiredly at his words, realising he'd nailed Anthony on the head. Her brother was indeed always bright, always bubbly, always eager to see the good in absolutely everything. She wasn't quite sure whether that was due to the

Down's syndrome or whether that was just Anthony's natural personality shining through. She liked to think it was a mixture of both as Anthony wouldn't be Anthony without the DS.

'Yes. Good thinking.'

'Then, perhaps later tonight, we could have dinner?' Gil's tone was polite yet intimate. 'Nothing fancy but perhaps a bit better than train food.'

William clicked his pen and made another notation in his file. 'I'll arrange dinner for two just down the road. Not that you dining together is any sort of secret, you understand, but I think it's best to—'

'Stop!' Phemie closed her eyes for a moment then shook her head. She looked at Gil as she spoke. 'I don't want to go to dinner tonight. I'm tired. I'm grubby. I'm uncomfortable. I've spent too long on a train, stressing about my brother and not getting much sleep.' The latter being all Gil's fault as she hadn't stopped thinking about him. 'And now with this accident and Mary and…' She trailed off and collected herself, calming her frantic tone.

'Thank you for the invitation, Gil, but this time I'll have to say, no, thanks. I think for the duration of the conference we need to keep everything strictly business. I'll let you know what happens with the RFDS request after I've spoken to my boss but apart from that—' Phemie held out her hand to him and tried not to gasp at the warmth that flooded through her as he slipped his hand into hers. 'Uh…thank you for the lift, thank you for an interesting train journey and uh…I hope you enjoy the conference and any sightseeing you get to do while you're in Sydney.'

The chauffeur had stopped the car and the hotel doorman was opening the passenger door. Gil didn't let go of Phemie's hand as he unbuckled both their seat belts, then climbed from the car, helping her out as he went.

He raised her hand gallantly to his lips and placed a sweet kiss on her skin. 'I'll have your luggage sent up to your room. Save you waiting around for it.'

'Uh…thank you.' Phemie tried not to blush, tried not to capitulate, tried not to throw herself into his arms and beg to have his mouth pressed to her lips rather than her hand. Why, when she was trying to keep things professional, when she was attempting to put some much-needed distance between them, did he go and do something like romantically kiss her hand? He was pure charm and when he aimed it in her direction, she was powerless to resist. However, she stilled the fluttering in her stomach and ordered her knees to stand firm, rather than collapsing into a heap right in front of him.

He let her hand go and it fell lifelessly back to her side. She needed to move. She needed to get out of there. Strong resolve. *Strong resolve!* It was what she must continue building if she was going to be spending more time with Gil once the conference was over. Strong resolve.

CHAPTER SEVEN

IT HAD been an excessively long day and Phemie was pleased she'd followed through on her whim to soak in a bubble bath. To have that sort of luxury was rare in her life, especially as in the outback water was more precious than gold.

Afterwards, she'd slipped into her pyjamas and sat on the big comfortable bed, flicking through the television channels. She'd called Anthony as soon as she'd arrived in her room, knowing it would be nigh on impossible to truly relax unless she was sure her brother was all right.

He'd talked animatedly about his day and that he'd not only seen the Sydney Harbour Bridge but that their bus had driven across it. Next, they'd visited the Opera House and had had their photograph taken on the steps with the Opera House in the background.

Phemie felt a little jealous. He'd not only had a much better day than her but he'd seen some of the classic Sydney icons. The most she would get to see whilst she was there was probably the inside of this very hotel.

She continued changing channels with a despondent air until she found she was back at the beginning. 'Hopeless,' she murmured, and switched the television off. She should be tired. She should be utterly exhausted and she was, but at the moment she simply couldn't seem to settle down. Sleep, it seemed, was going to evade her once more.

Picking up her mobile phone, she called through to the Didja RFDS base and managed to catch Ben just before he left for the day.

'Don't tell me you're bored,' he joked.

'A little,' she confessed to her friend. 'But I'm also really tired.'

'Then either go to sleep or go out and see a bit of the city. You're going to be stuck in that hotel for the next three days so take the time to get out while you still can.'

'You make it sound like an asylum.'

'It's a hotel. It's a box. Give me wide open spaces and fresh air any day.'

Phemie sighed. 'I know what you mean.' She paused. 'Also, while I have you on the phone, can you give me an update on Kiefer?'

'Ah...I knew it. You rang to find out about a patient, rather than ringing because you've missed your ol' mate.'

'No. That's not true at all. I miss you. All of you.'

'Well, if you weren't such a brilliant doctor who wrote such a brilliant paper, you wouldn't have been chosen to present your findings along with all the other brilliant medics in the nation.'

'You are so long-winded. An update, please?'

'The reattachment operation went well, as you already know, and his post-operative recovery has been non-eventful.'

'Good. I needed some good news.'

'Bad day?'

Phemie was almost about to tell Ben about Mary and the car crash when there was a knock at her hotel door. 'Hang on, Ben. Won't be a moment.' Phemie went to the door and checked through the peephole to see who was standing outside the door, expecting it to be someone who had gone to the wrong room.

'Gil.' His name was a whisper, her eyes widening in surprise. What did he want? She'd received her luggage, so what more could the man want? He was standing patiently, hands behind his back, waiting for her to open the door.

She was trying desperately to make sure there was a professional distance between them and he was making that increasingly difficult when he kept bumping into her or offering a lift or coming to her hotel room to see her. Didn't the man understand she wasn't interested in any sort of relationship with him? Well, obviously, she wanted to keep on reading his articles and following his research breakthroughs but that was it. They were both doctors. He was more qualified, more experienced, more everything than her.

Being near him, having him standing close to her, looking into his eyes, remembering how it felt to be in his arms, the subtle spicy scent he wore drove her to distraction every time he was beside her. It was all becoming too much to fight but fight it she must.

There was no room in her life to have these feelings, these growing emotions for a man she would never be able to be with. She'd chosen her path, made her decision never to get married and have children, and she would stick with it. Helping people was what she did best and she'd proven that today when she'd helped Mary. And then Gil had helped her by supporting her when she'd broken down and cried.

Now he was waiting for her to open the door. The sooner she did, the sooner she could find out what he wanted and the sooner she could send him on his way. She could simply stand there at the door, he didn't even need to come into the room. Did he? No. He didn't.

Resolution made, she reached out her hand, pleased to find it firm and steady, and opened the weighted hotel door.

'Gil.' She didn't move out of the way, didn't invite him in.

'Euphemia.' His smile was warm and polite but this time it didn't meet his eyes. A niggling sensation started to rumble in her stomach as she stood there and watched him for another second.

'I'm on the phone,' she finally remarked when he didn't say anything more. Had he come all the way from the lofty heights of the suite he was staying in down to the fifth floor just to stand at her door and say her name?

'Sorry. I didn't mean to intrude.' Still he didn't move or walk away. 'May I come in?'

Why had he asked? She'd been doing such a good job of keeping her distance but now it would seem churlish to refuse. 'Sure.' Phemie moved aside, holding the door as he walked into her room. She lifted the mobile to her ear. 'I'll talk to you later, Ben. Bye.' She disconnected the call.

'I'm sorry to intrude, Phemie.' He looked at her bright print pyjamas, only then realising she was dressed for bed. When she'd opened the door, he'd been so captured by her hair, which she'd recently washed, as it bounced around her shoulders, the blonde tendrils curling a little at the ends. Her skin was fresh and clear of all make-up, and she'd never looked more beautiful. Phemie's beauty was natural, radiating from within, and he knew that was the main reason he was so captivated by her.

Still, he hadn't come simply to stare. That would be truly dangerous, as staring at Phemie only led him to want to touch her, and if he touched her then he'd want to kiss her, and whilst he'd thought about that quite a bit in the past couple of days, wondering how it would feel with his mouth pressed to hers, he knew following through on that whim would be foolish as well as downright mean to both of them. They lived worlds apart—literally.

'What do you want, Gil?' She was tired and she wasn't in the mood to play games, especially when it appeared he was just going to stand there, looking at her as though he was ready to devour her. She put her guard up, knowing she needed to keep a level head.

'Uh…yes. Sorry. There is a specific reason why I'm intruding on your evening. I'm afraid I have some bad news.'

Phemie's annoyance with him instantly disappeared and her breathing paused for a moment as her mind sorted through the reasons why Gil would come to her room bearing bad news. It didn't take too long to realise the answer. 'Mary.'

'Yes.' Gil shoved his hands into his pockets to stop himself from reaching for her. The look on her face was one of resigned acceptance, as though she'd known the odds hadn't been in Mary's favour. There was pain there, concern and also a look of defeat. It couldn't be the first patient she'd ever lost but he knew from experience that some people, despite how long you'd known them, could leave a lasting imprint on your life when they passed away. It appeared, for Phemie, Mary had been such a person.

'When?'

'The surgeon called me about ten minutes ago. She didn't make it through the operation.'

Phemie looked blankly at the light-coloured curtains, which she'd pulled closed earlier. The room was decorated in bland nondescript colours and that was how she felt right now. Bland and nondescript.

Gil could do nothing except watch her and wait. There was pain in her eyes. Those beautiful blue eyes which had been so vibrant in the past were now dull as they stared unseeingly past him.

'The surgeon called you?'

It hadn't been what he'd expected her to say but as she met his gaze, Gil nodded and took a hand from his pocket to rub it across the side of his temple. 'William tracked down the surgeon before he went into Theatre with Mary and told him I wanted to be kept informed of all progress.'

'I guess the name Professor Fitzwilliam carries more weight than I thought.'

Gil shrugged, not apologising for who he was. 'I knew you'd want to know, hence my intrusion.' He nodded politely, inclining his head so it was almost a bow. 'I'll leave you to your solitude now.' With that, he headed for the door but stopped when he heard her voice.

'I was probably the last person to just chat with Mary.' Phemie breathed deeply, unevenly, as though she was trying to control her emotions. 'It's ridiculous really. I hardly knew the woman and yet she's left a lasting impression on me. We talked. We chatted as though we were long-lost friends. There was no awkwardness. She was so open, so eager to tell me about her parents and Daniel. Two of her best friends had just died in that same crash and yet the way she spoke of them was with happiness and love.'

Phemie obviously needed to unwind, to say these things, to share Mary with someone else. Quietly, he walked back into the room and sat down, still keeping his distance. Being there to support her was one thing and he was more than happy to do that, but getting involved with her was quite out of the question.

She rubbed the back of her neck, massaging the area gently. 'I was only doing my job. I was talking to Mary to keep her lucid, to ensure she stayed awake, and yet she was having the last real conversation of her life.' Phemie swallowed over the sudden lump in her throat. 'I've come to realise how wrong I've been.'

'About?'

'Anthony. Listening to Mary talk about Daniel and how they were good friends...' Phemie stopped and shook her head. 'I've always wanted that, you see. I love Anthony but at the same time

I've always yearned to have a real sibling relationship. Brother and sister. Arguing. Laughing. Doing things together. I always felt cheated that I never had that and now Mary's made me realise it's my fault. I could have had that with Anthony if I'd only worked harder, seen him in a different light, not been so bothered about other "perfect" families and how they all interacted.' Tears dropped from her lashes and slid slowly down her cheeks.

'You are a *great* sister, Phemie,' Gil said. 'From what I heard of your conversations with Mary, and I don't want you to think I was eavesdropping, but her brother was much younger than her. That in itself makes a big difference. When you were telling her about Anthony, every time you mentioned his name, there was a deep, abiding love in your tone. You may not have had the relationship you *imagined* you wanted but you have a very solid relationship with him all the same. Sure, it may seem more like parent to child rather than sibling to sibling but that doesn't mean it's wrong or invalid. You shared yourself with Mary and I have to say, you're quite a woman. Not everyone can do that. You were open with her, telling her about your brother, your parents and about yourself, how you'd been afraid to leave your job at Perth hospital to move to Didja but that you're very glad you did. I heard you telling her how much you like helping people and that's when she thanked you for being there to help her.' Gil kept his words soft but firm, wanting to get cross to Phemie that she had not only listened to Mary, that she'd not only provided first-rate medical care, but that she'd also *given* that dying woman respect by treating her normally.

'The last thing Mary needed whilst she was trapped was to panic. You kept her sane, made her feel as though she was strong enough to pull through it.'

'But I knew she wasn't.' The words burst forth from Phemie like a rocket and she covered her face with her hands. 'I knew she wasn't going to make it. I just knew it yet I kept on giving her hope. False hope.'

'You're a doctor. You do what's in the best interests of your patient.'

Phemie dropped her hands and walked to the tissues, yanking one out and blowing her nose loudly. Where was the man who had held her so tenderly that afternoon? The one who had put his big strong arms around her, making her feel safe and secure? Where was he now? She needed him.

Instead, she appeared to be faced with a doctor who was giving her clinical and logical answers about why she was so bereft at Mary's passing.

'Even lying to them in their last moments?'

'Yes.' Gil stood and strode towards her, clasping her arms with his hands. He wanted to give her a good shake but remained firm. 'This wasn't your fault. Mary's death wasn't your fault. You did everything you could and much, much more for her, and you need to accept that.'

'What if I can't?' She looked up at him. The desire to feel his arms about her, rather than firmly holding her at a distance, was what she wanted more than anything right now. She knew it wasn't right. She knew she shouldn't want him as much as she did but, having felt his arms around her before, she wanted that sensation, that feeling of being protected, of being cared for, to envelop her and wash away the pain.

'You have to. You're a professional.'

His words seemed harsh and she didn't want to hear them. 'She was my friend.'

'No. She was a patient. Someone who needed your help. She was a woman you met. A nice young woman who has had an impact on your life. You need to deal with it and move on.'

Phemie could feel her anger rising at his words. She was hurting, she was in pain and all he could do was spout platitudes about emotions he obviously knew nothing about. He may be a genius but it appeared he had no idea about feeling empathy for a person who had passed away. He was being cold and professional and the more he was like that, the angrier she became. She didn't like his rationalised reasoning. She knew the psychology but it didn't help the way she felt. She knew she needed to pull herself together, and she would—later—but right now she wanted to mourn for Mary and she'd foolishly hoped Gil would share her sentiments. Obviously, she'd been wrong.

With a quick move, she brought both her hands up between his and pushed them out to the side, effectively breaking his hold on her. 'I know what I need to do and I don't appreciate your attempts to psychoanalyse my emotions away. I'm upset, Gil. Someone I liked, someone I'm proud to call my friend, has just died and you're wanting me to be rational about this?

'Well, Professor, let me tell you that sometimes people need to be irrational. They need to do what's not expected. If I want to wallow, if I want to mope around and cry and be upset for a woman who at the age of twenty-one has had her life ripped from her, then I shall cry and be upset, despite how little I knew her. Our acquaintance may have been short but it was filled with special moments. Quality, not quantity. And she may have been just a patient in the beginning but by the end she was a woman I admired.'

'Phemie, I—'

She pushed past him and walked to the door, opening it, indicating he should leave. It was necessary that he go. Her yearning for his arms around her, her yearning for him to understand her emotions, her yearning for him to simply be there for her was becoming too much to deal with on top of everything else. She wanted to lean on him, to have him support her, but she also knew if she did that, if he offered that, it would only enhance the growing addiction she felt for him.

'Look, I understand you've had a very rough and long few days.'

'Yeah.' She laughed without humour. 'You've got that right, which is why you're leaving.'

'I didn't come here to upset you. I simply wanted to inform you—in person—about—'

'And I appreciate it. However, I'd also appreciate it if you'd just leave me alone.'

There was a certain look in her eyes as she said the words and Gil realised she wasn't just talking about the absent-minded way he'd handled himself in the past ten minutes. She was hurt, she was tired and he could see she really did want to be left alone. Not only that, he understood she also wanted him to keep his distance on a personal level. It was difficult, especially when she was wearing such cute pyjamas, making her look all snuggly and warm. Did she have any idea how alluring she was, how he was having such a difficult time keeping his hands to himself?

She was right, though. He should go. He should leave her alone. He wasn't quite sure why he continued to seek her out, why he continued to think of her so often, but he would endeavour to do as she now asked.

'Of course. My sincerest apologies, Euphemia.'

His clipped accented tones washed over her as he once more inclined his head in the polite way she'd come to equate with him before walking calmly through her open doorway. Out in the hallway once more, he turned before she could close the door.

'I do hope you manage to sleep well,' he murmured, before walking off towards the lifts and doing what she'd asked all along—leaving her alone.

* * *

Phemie was a little on edge the next morning. Although the conference didn't officially begin until Monday, Sunday had been set aside for conference speakers and presenters to not only get to know each other but also to be first in line to attend the Trade shows which would open later that afternoon to the rest of the conference delegates. As such, it was a full day's programme which began with a welcome breakfast in one of the smaller, more intimate conference rooms, where she came face to face with Gil.

'Good morning, Euphemia.'

'Professor.' She nodded politely as she scooped some strawberries onto her plate, ignoring the way her heart rate increased its usual rhythm.

'I trust you were able to sleep well?'

'Yes, thank you.'

With that, Phemie smiled, even though it didn't reach her eyes, and took her plate back to her seat. As she sat down, she made sure she didn't watch him to see what else he did or who else he spoke to.

'Do you know Professor Fitzwilliam?' Another presenter who was sitting at her table asked.

'Not really.' Which was true. What did she really know about Gil except that he was a brilliant specialist, was English and had the most hypnotic eyes she'd ever gazed into? The fact that he could set her heart racing with a simple look meant nothing. Or that he could make her knees weaken with the briefest of touches, or that being in the same room as him made her mind turn to mush. No. None of it meant a thing. Keeping her distance, protecting herself was the better thing to focus on.

She had almost finished her breakfast when the conference co-ordinator stood and tapped on the side of his glass for quiet. Soon everyone was paying attention.

'Welcome, presenters,' the female co-ordinator began, before launching into a rundown of the day's activities. 'First of all, though, I have the honour, nay, the pleasure…' she looked down at the front table where Gil sat and smiled brightly at him, almost *too* brightly, Phemie thought '…of introducing one of the world's leading experts in emergency medicine.' She continued by listing a long string of Gil's qualifications and achievements, before turning the podium over to him.

Amid a round of applause Gil took to the podium, dressed neatly in his three-piece pinstripe suit, where he looked every inch the revered professor he was. Phemie contrasted him to the man she'd met on the train and found they were vastly different. Even the way he spoke was different, his rich warm tones washing over her, his accent far more pronounced then in the quiet moments they'd shared together before Kiefer's accident.

Why did all of that—the journey on the train— seem so long ago? Why did it feel as though she *had* known Gil for more than a couple of days? Was it because she'd read so many of his articles she felt as though she really *did* know him? Or was it the frightening natural chemistry that seemed to exist between them?

Gil calmly scanned the room as he spoke. A smattering of laughter broke out and it was then Phemie realised she'd missed whatever little anecdote he'd just related. When his gaze settled on her she felt like a deer caught in the headlights of an oncoming car. Even across the room, it was as though his brown eyes devoured her and her breathing rapidly increased.

It was only a moment, just a brief flash of time, yet once again she felt completely encompassed by him. It was as though he'd been quietly search- ing the crowded room for her and her alone. Now that he'd found her, he couldn't be bothered paying anyone else attention.

Phemie looked down. Breaking the contact.

Unable to endure the intense moment any longer. She forced herself to pick up her toast, to take a bite, to do something—anything—to get her mind off the man at the front of the room. When she realised her hand was trembling, she immediately put the toast back and clasped her hands in her lap, squeezing them together so tightly she thought she might snap a bone.

She wasn't able to look at Gil for the rest of his speech and at the first available opportunity she politely excused herself and made her way to the ladies room. Her heart was still pounding, her hands were still trembling and when she glanced at her reflection in the mirror, she was astonished at how wild and bright her eyes appeared.

Her blonde hair was pulled back into a chignon, she was wearing a navy skirt, white shirt and matching navy jacket. She looked every inch the professional yet she felt far from it. One look from Gil and she'd ended up a mass of schoolgirl tingles, unable to control her own body's reaction.

Deciding it was best to simply skip the rest of the welcome breakfast and return to her room until it was time for the trade show, Phemie exited the ladies room and headed for the bank of elevators. She didn't look back but instead focused on her escape from a man she simply couldn't stop thinking about.

When was she going to find some self-control? Relationships weren't for her. She knew that and it was a decision she herself had made years ago. Letting the way Gil made her feel rule her life would only mean she'd not only end up alone but miserable as well. If only he wasn't so attractive, so endearing, so…on her wavelength.

He was a doctor, which meant he understood the working hours she had to endure, he was great with his patients and most of all he'd been incredible with Anthony. She often judged people on how they treated her brother, especially given most new acquaintances were a little taken aback when they found out Anthony had a disability. Gil, however, had treated Anthony like a long-lost friend and the picture of the two of them sitting at the table on the train, laughing together, brought an instant smile to her face.

These facts only made Gil more dangerous, only made it even more necessary for her to avoid him wherever possible, especially during the next couple of days. When he returned with her to the Didja base, she would keep her distance and play the polite host to perfection. Gil might even want to go and spend a few days working with her good friend Dex. That would mean less time she had to tiptoe around the issue that she wanted nothing more than to hold him close and never let him go.

At that thought alone, Phemie closed her eyes, not wanting to think about him any more, about how he was affecting her and also about just how deep her feelings for him seemed to be developing. Even if she did, *could*, admit to herself that Gil might turn out to be someone special, someone she really wanted to spend time with, there was also the added complication of geography.

No. There wasn't any way that any sort of real relationship could prosper.

CHAPTER EIGHT

AT THE end of the day, Phemie flicked off her shoes and slumped down on to the bed, rubbing her feet. She was not used to wearing high heels and her toes were now starting to complain. She changed into more comfortable clothes, jeans and a burgundy knit top, before picking up the TV remote and lounging on the bed, luxuriating in the soft furnishings which she definitely didn't have back on the RFDS base.

The phone rang and she quickly switched the set off before answering the call. 'Dr Grainger.' Only after she'd picked up the receiver did she think it might be Gil, and a wild flutter filled her stomach whilst at the same time she dreaded knowing what she ought to say to him.

'Oh, yes…um…' The voice was female and hesitant. 'I'm sorry to bother you, Doctor. I'm, uh…Carren Milton. Mary's mother.'

Phemie gasped, pain rushing through her again,

but she pushed it aside, knowing she needed to be strong, to pass on the information Mary had wanted her parents to know. 'Mrs Milton. Thank you for calling me.'

'I understand you were with Mary at the… the—'

'I was,' Phemie interrupted. 'She asked me to call you.'

'Oh.' Mrs Milton was close to tears and Phemie was having a difficult time controlling her own.

'She wanted me to tell you about my brother, Anthony.'

When the phone call ended, Phemie felt better about Mary and she started to feel the faint stirrings of peace. She looked around the small, impersonal hotel room and shook her head.

'No.' The walls felt as though they were about to close in. She was a woman who was used to wide open spaces and at the moment, feeling a little unnerved, she needed somewhere more open than this. Slipping on a pair of flat shoes and grabbing her room key, she headed down to the lobby.

'Better,' she murmured as she found an empty wing-backed chair in the hotel's French-themed café-bar. A waiter came over but she told him she wasn't ready to order anything just yet. He left her alone and she closed her eyes, finally starting to relax.

'Hello.'

At the rich, deep tones she recognised all too well, she opened her eyes and looked up to find Gil standing opposite her.

'Professor.' She tried to make her tone sound more tired as she shifted in the chair. 'I hope you haven't come to deliver more bad news?'

'Er…no.'

Phemie couldn't help allowing her gaze to wander over him and it was difficult not to be affected by his more casual attire of jeans and jumper—not that he didn't look incredibly handsome in a suit. He most certainly did but before her was the man she'd come to know on the train, rather than the medical genius. That thought alone relaxed her a little bit…but only a little. 'Is there something I can help you with?'

'I do believe we had a date to have tea together.'

Phemie stared at him for a moment, her fuzzy mind trying to comprehend his words. 'Oh, tea—drinking tea rather than eating tea. Yes. Oh, I'm sorry, Gil. I'd completely forgotten.' Her annoyance with him started to dissipate. Maybe it was his casual attire, maybe it was the calm look in his gorgeous eyes, maybe it was that she was just too tired to be defensive. 'I was going to find a tea house and I—' She stopped, sighing and pushing her hand through her loose blonde locks. 'I'm sorry.'

'You're exhausted.' She may not have invited him to sit down but at least she was back to calling him by his first name. He decided to take a chance and force his hand by sitting in the chair opposite. When she made no comment, he signalled the waiter.

'Two teas, please,' he ordered. The waiter nodded and went to walk away but Gil hadn't finished. 'I'd like Australian tea if you have it. Something rich in body and full in flavour, and if it's at all possible to get it in a pot with some proper bone china cups, I'd thoroughly appreciate it.'

'I'll see what I can do, sir,' the waiter replied, before leaving them.

When he looked over at Phemie, she was smiling and slowly shaking her head. 'Something wrong?' he asked.

'You're so…English,' she said with a chuckle, and he joined in.

'Thank you. I'll take that as a compliment.' He didn't care where they went to have a cup of tea together, at least he was finally going to get some one-on-one time with the woman who seemed to have invaded his thoughts. The area in which they sat wasn't overly crowded and he was pleased. He'd been in two minds whether to come and see her this evening, to force her hand in remembering their date, especially after what had happened last night and earlier this morning at the breakfast. It was clear she was tired but he really wanted to spend time with her, and after telling William he wasn't available for any tête-a-têtes this evening, he'd headed quietly from his suite and made his way to the lobby, surprised to have found her there.

While they waited for their drinks, they chatted about the conference sessions and she praised him for his speech, even though she hadn't really been paying attention to most of it, given she'd been too distracted by him.

'You mentioned when we first met that you would like me to have a look at your presentation. Is that still the case?' Gil asked after their tea had been delivered. He allowed it to brew before pouring two cups.

'I would but I don't—' She stopped and shook her head. 'You no doubt have better things to do. Besides, if you gave private lessons to every delegate, we'd never get through the conference!'

'Let me worry about my workload and you are not

"every delegate", Phemie.' He looked into his cup for a moment before meeting her eyes. 'You're a friend.'

'Am I?' Phemie picked up her cup of tea and took a sip, needing to do something other than gaze into his eyes and lose all rational thought. She leaned her head into the side of the chair and closed her eyes, a furrow marring her brow. 'I'm so confused.'

'Mmm.' He couldn't agree more but decided not to voice his thoughts. It was true that he regarded her as a friend, as someone he wanted to care for, to spend time with, but confessing more than that wouldn't be wise, he felt.

She opened her eyes and stared at him. 'We hardly know each other, Gil.'

'Are we not trying to rectify that? We're sitting here, drinking tea and talking, finding out more about what makes the other one tick.' He sat forward in the chair and looked at her. 'I like hot Indian curries and the take-away shop makes them much better than I ever could. However, I prefer to cook my own roast dinner.'

'You cook?'

'I do and very well, thank you very much. What else can I tell you about me?' He thought for a second before a glint touched his eyes. 'I drive an old jalopy which was the very first car I bought when I was seventeen. I've lovingly restored it and enjoy keeping it in tip-top shape.' It was also the one place he'd found a bit of peace and happiness after the tragedy that robbed him of his family. He paused and sipped his tea, a far-off look in his eyes.

'You've missed your car?' Phemie's smile was one of surprise that Gil was displaying an emotional connection to an inanimate object. It was right. It grounded him. Made him seem more… normal.

He smiled longingly. 'I have. It's about all I'm looking forward to when I return to England.'

'Really? Your car? You can't do any better than that? Can't think of any other reasons why you want to go home after a year of travelling the globe?' She knew he was no doubt joking yet when she looked into his eyes it was to find them filled with sadness and regret.

'No.'

Phemie watched, waiting for him to expand his answer, but he remained silent. She put her cup down as her heart went out to him. 'Oh, Gil. Really? No family? Friends? Surely you have a great job waiting for you?'

'Not really. And friends…' He shrugged. 'I've made some great friends whilst travelling.'

'Like William?'

His smile was instant but it was nowhere near as bright or as relaxed as before. 'William and I have become friends, yes. It's difficult not to when spending so much time working together. That goes for the rest of the people who have assisted me on this fellowship.' He shook his head. 'In some ways it feels like yesterday the fellowship began but most of the time it feels like I've been travelling for ever.'

'Were you stuck in a rut? Is that why you decided on the fellowship?' Phemie put her hand up to stop him. 'Sorry. That was a little personal. You don't have to answer that. It was ru—'

'My wife died.' The words were out before he could stop them. He didn't talk to just anyone about his past yet somehow he had the instinctive feeling that Phemie was the right person. Ever since they'd met he'd felt such a natural yet deep connection with her. He'd read sadness in her eyes as well as struggle and hardship. Knowing she had a brother with a disability also meant her life had been filled with compromises…just as his had been.

Phemie gasped and put her hand over her mouth. 'Oh, no, Gil.'

'She died four years ago in a plane crash. It was one of those random things that happen. She was returning from Italy, after seeing her family, and the plane just…' Gil trailed off, his words spoken very matter-of-factly. It was as though if he put emotion into the words, it would make it more real. Instead, he related the information like a medical professional in order to distance himself from the pain. 'She died instantly, at least that's what they told me.' That had brought him little comfort because he could well imagine the panic she must have felt prior to the impact. It was also the reason he loathed flying. It was one of the hurdles he'd had to overcome when he'd accepted the fellowship and even though he'd been successful, he still preferred an alternative if possible. Hence he'd chosen to travel from Perth to Sydney via train.

Slowly, Phemie shook her head. 'Gil. No wonder you wanted to get away, to do the fellowship. How did you survive those initial years?'

'Work. Locked myself in and threw away the key. I started to realise it was time I reconnected properly with the human race and I couldn't do that trapped in an office behind a desk, researching and writing articles.'

'Ah.' Dawning realisation crossed Phemie's face. 'That's why you've been so prolific.'

'Exactly. Although I have to say that writing all those articles made it easier for me to not only secure the fellowship, it's also helped introduce me to a lot of very interesting people.' He looked pointedly at her and she smiled. 'People who I bump into on…oh, let's say trains, and they instantly recognise me.'

Phemie's smile increased and she shrugged. 'They were good articles. You have a natural flair for the written word and you explain new techniques with ease.'

'Says the woman who has such an impressive list of credentials she could be running a busy city hospital's A and E department yet is stationed with the RFDS in the Australian outback.' The look he gave her was one of admiration.

She started to defend her decision to move, not wanting him to know she'd gone to the outback as a way of trying desperately to find herself. She'd all but forced herself out of her very comfortable comfort zone and Didja was where she'd ended up. 'They need the help and it's difficult to get doctors in remote— Wait.' Realisation crossed her face. 'What do you mean "impressive list of credentials"? How do you know about my qualifications?'

Gil looked at his cup for a second before meeting Phemie's gaze. 'I...uh...have dossiers on all the conference presenters.'

'You do?'

'Yes. It's supposed to be a way of letting me know more about you so that when we meet and chat, I'm not completely in the dark. I guess, in a way, it makes me look good because everyone thinks I know what's going on.'

'And do you?'

He chuckled but there wasn't a lot of humour in it. In that instant Phemie had the inkling that he was more than done with this travelling fellowship. Too many countries, too many speeches, too many doctors to compliment and encourage. 'Not really.'

Gil put his cup down and leaned forward in his chair. 'I have to confess, though, that when I first received the dossiers, I sifted through them until I found yours.' He shrugged a shoulder. 'I just wanted to know more about you.'

'You did?' Her eyes widened at this and Gil stood, shifting his chair closer to hers.

'I've wanted to know more about you since the moment I bumped into you on the train.' The memory of her body close to his as people had passed them in those very narrow corridors came instantly to mind and a powerful heat spread through him.

'Oh.' She seemed to be saying that a lot tonight but she simply couldn't help herself. It wasn't only his declaration she was dealing with but the fact that he'd moved closer. Now his scent was winding itself around her, making her forget everything except the way he made her feel when he was close enough to touch. Heat was radiating out from his thigh, which wasn't too far from her leg, and she immediately shifted, crossing her legs beneath her and trying to edge back into the far corner of the huge chair.

'You've intrigued me from the first moment I met you, Euphemia Grainger.' His gaze was firm on hers as he leaned a little closer.

'Uh…hmm.' She kept her eyes trained on the top of his open-necked polo shirt, finding it increasingly difficult to meet his gaze. In the past few days his eyes had managed to have a hypnotic effect on her and right now, here, in this secluded corner of the hotel's café-bar, the two of them alone, she needed to hold onto every shred of sanity she could muster. 'Uh…and what have you…er…you know…discovered?'

'About you?'

'Yes.'

'For a start, you're one smart lady.'

'Oh. Thank you.' She swallowed, the tension within her mounting because she *felt* rather than *knew* something big was about to happen.

'Today's proceedings were all about the presenters having the opportunity to get to know each other and their keynote speaker before the conference really begins tomorrow.' His words were even, spoken in his normal tone, yet there was a definite undercurrent in the deep, resonant sound. 'I've had a day of talking, of relating, of smiling and making inconsequential remarks.'

'Mmm-hmm.' Phemie was watching his lips as he spoke, the tension in her still continuing to climb.

'Yet throughout it all, I kept thinking about one presenter in particular. One presenter who I haven't been able to stop thinking about.'

Phemie couldn't control the butterflies that were going crazy within her. His words were so soft, so gentle, so incredible to hear. Did he have any idea how wonderful his words made her feel? How special? Gil was admitting that he was thinking about her when he shouldn't be, that she had distracted him from his work, and whilst she felt a smidgen of guilt, her heart soared with elation.

'Uh...huh...I...um, know the feeling.' Why did her voice sound so husky? So intimate? So...not like her at all. Phemie glanced up at him, needing to exhale a little as her breathing was become more erratic with each passing second. 'Gil?'

'Yes?'

Phemie's smile was small but personal. Gil liked it—a lot. 'I think I'm getting to know the keynote speaker much better right now.'

'Yes.' It was then he saw it. That look of acceptance in her eyes. Previously, she'd been hard-pressed to even look him in the eyes, instead preferring to examine the top of his chest. 'Phemie?'

'Mmm?' Her heart was pounding so forcefully against her chest she was positive it was about to damage her ribs.

'Is this OK?'

'Huh?' What was he asking her? And how on earth did he expect her to be able to comprehend anything at the moment? Especially when he was looking at her as though he wanted to devour her.

'Me. Being here.'

'Here?' Her breathing was uneven and her gaze

kept flicking between his eyes and his mouth, the intense awareness continuing to build and grow.

'With you.' He smiled and it was almost her undoing.

'It's, uh…' Her tongue snaked out to wet her lips as she sighed. 'It's fine. Whatever it is that I'm saying is fine because I can't think much right now,' she babbled.

'I know the feeling.' Gil reached out a hand and caressed her cheek, amazed at how perfectly soft her skin felt. 'You are incredibly beautiful.'

Her mouth formed a little 'O' but no sound came out. Instead, she licked her lips again, needing to wet them because of her heavier than normal breathing.

'I've wanted to kiss you for so long.' He cupped her cheek, Phemie's breath catching at his touch. He leaned in further, his breath fanning her face as he spoke, oh so softly. It was intoxicating having him this close!

'I've thought about it a lot,' he continued. 'About how your mouth would feel against mine. About how you would taste. About how, if I allow myself to follow through on such an impulsive action, I'd be opening Pandora's box.'

At hearing these words, words which were spoken with depth and emotion, Phemie started to tremble. He found her attractive? He wanted to kiss her? If he followed through on the action, what did it mean? What would happen next? She was so used to having her life all neatly mapped out before her and yet from the moment she'd met Gil, her schedule had been thrown into disarray.

Kissing him was what she wanted. It was what she'd thought about and she'd rationalised that it was OK, mainly because she hadn't expected him to be doing the same thing. She simply hadn't expected a man like Gil, with his knowledge of the world, with his experience, with his standing in the medical community, to want someone like her. Yet he'd just declared as much and there was truth in his looks.

'Gil.' His name was a caress on her lips and it was all he needed. That final moment of acceptance, that she was ready for this to happen. Was he, though? This would be the first woman he'd romantically kissed since his wife, June.

He looked at Phemie's lips. Parted, pink and ready for him. He was about to kiss another woman and it felt right. It felt *so* right.

Phemie's head was spinning. She was about to be kissed by a man, something that hadn't happened to her in a very long time. Something she wasn't sure she was ready for, but by the same token if he stopped now, she was sure she'd self-combust from anticipation alone.

'Phemie.' Her name was barely audible on his lips but as his mesmerising gaze dipped from her eyes to her mouth, she swallowed. She was ready. She was willing and she was more than able to fulfil her fantasy of kissing him.

Within the next second his mouth was on hers, and she slowly released the breath she hadn't even been conscious of holding. Neither of them moved for that first incredible moment, wanting to absorb all the sensations surrounding them.

He cupped her cheek, angling her head towards him, holding her in place as he savoured her flavours. So sweet, so tender, so fresh. The woman was everything he'd imagined and more. As he parted her lips, he found her a willing participant, eager to go with him on this journey, to attempt to discover exactly what this thing was that existed between them.

Still, he knew he needed to keep his self-control completely in check. He wasn't ready for anything more than this and neither was she. This attraction between them had sprung up out of nowhere and whilst they were both acknowledging it, the fact remained that he didn't live in this country and he wasn't the type of man to use a woman for his own needs.

The sensations, the explosions of fireworks that seemed to fill the room as his mouth continued to explore hers were definitely unexpected. Although his touch was soft, delicate and to the point of being so light she could barely feel it at times, Phemie was too scared to move in case he stopped. She didn't want him to stop. The unhurried exploration of each other gave every emotion time to pass through her before exploding in a blaze of light. She felt as though she was floating, dizzy, giddy on the intoxication that was Gil.

The sensations were so refined, so minute, so intimate. His hand was warm at her cheek with only the slightest pressure to keep her close, and as she leaned into his touch, she heard him moan with repressed hunger.

Slowly, he edged back. The energy, the needs were intensifying and the fact that he was in a hotel, his mouth on hers, not even sure what his name was any more, was an indication that things had just become very complicated. Self-control. He needed to remain in control of the situation. If he remained in control of his faculties then he could cope with this mild flirtation—because that's all it could ever be. At least, that's what he needed to tell himself.

With one last taste, Gil eased back, his thumb rubbing almost imperceptibly across her cheek before he slowly removed his hand, unable to brush his fingers across her slightly swollen lips. She kept her eyes closed as her breathing returned to normal and as he sat there, looking at her, marvelling at just how beautiful she was, he was hard-pressed not to return his mouth to hers for a second kiss. The urge to throw caution to the wind was starting to overpower him.

He had to retreat before he risked causing them both pain.

He stood so abruptly he almost knocked the table over and moved away, striving to put distance between them whilst he regained control over his faculties. Phemie watched him, saw the look of determination on his face and came to the conclusion that Gil was now regretting what had just happened between them. Pain shot through her but she ignored it. Whilst she wanted him, and the kiss they'd just shared was total evidence of that, she had no room for him in her life.

Yes, they'd both been curious. Yes, they'd both

thought about it and, yes, the attraction was still very much there, buzzing between them, but sharing a kiss changed nothing. At least, that's what she told herself in order to put barriers up between them.

'Um…' She searched her mind, forcing her brain to switch back into gear. 'We don't need to go over the presentation.' She shifted uncomfortably, before standing, shifting so she was behind the large winged-back chair. 'I'll be fine.'

'Of course you will. You're a smart, intelligent woman.' His tone was more normal, more brisk, more *professor-ish*. Good. Perhaps this meant they were back on a more even keel and could, therefore, move forward as though nothing had happened.

'Thank you.'

'And thank you for sharing tea with me. It had a lot of flavour and tasted nothing like dishwater.' His smile was polite but it didn't reach his eyes. Both of them were avoiding the topic, the one that would take them back to a place they'd best leave alone. Their easygoing camaraderie had vanished yet the memory of what had transpired was still uppermost in both their minds.

'You're more than welcome.' The awkwardness was so thick you could have sliced it with a scalpel.

Gil took a step towards the exit. 'I'd best go. You need to get back to your room and sleep.'

'As do you. You have a far busier schedule than I do.'

'True. Well.' He nodded politely to her. 'I'll see you tomorrow, Euphemia.'

'Thank you, Professor.'

At the use of his title, Gil raised one eyebrow but didn't make any other comment. 'Goodnight,' he added, before turning and walking towards the main hotel lobby.

Slowly, as he walked towards the bank of lifts, the realisation of what had just happened hit him with full force. He'd kissed another woman. A woman who wasn't his wife. A woman who wasn't June.

The pain of losing his wife and daughter had torn his heart to shreds. He'd locked himself away. He'd focused on work. He'd had one person after another telling him that in time he would move on. That in time his heart would heal and that he'd one day be able to love again.

He hadn't believed them.

Now, though…he was torn with a mixture of emotions. Part of him was proud that he'd managed to take that step. That after four years he was not only interested in another woman but had actually kissed her. Yet the other part felt as though he'd betrayed June. He'd kissed another woman. He'd moved on with his life and he'd left June behind. She didn't deserve that.

He took the lift back to his suite, where he kicked off his shoes and lay down on the bed, hands behind his head as he looked at the ceiling. It had taken him years to get over June's death and until the moment he'd pressed his mouth to Phemie's, he hadn't thought he had. He'd had some idea that sackcloth and ashes would be the normal way of his life and yet, without realising it, he'd moved on.

He'd somehow moved away from needing June lying beside him in the bed, hearing little Caitie breathing from the crib. He'd sold their house, he'd bought an apartment in Bath, not far from the hospital, and he'd locked himself and his memories away.

To find that at some point during the past four years he'd unconsciously moved on left him feeling more than a little guilty. That part of him felt hollow whilst the other part, the part that could still taste and smell Phemie in glorious Technicolor, felt free and elated.

It was all completely ridiculous. He simply didn't do personal relationships. Not any more. They caused far too much pain when things, beyond your control, went wrong. Perhaps it would be a bad idea to go back to the RFDS base where she worked. Being that close to the woman, working alongside her, without too many distractions, seeing her smile, or the way she brushed her blonde hair out of her eyes, or...

'No.' He stopped the thoughts. Personal relationships were out of the question but from a medical perspective he was highly intrigued with the RFDS set-up. To be able to experience it first hand might even assist with his research. Work. Work was what he needed to focus on, not the soft, supple lips of Dr Grainger, yet when he closed his eyes again, the vision of her face was all he could see.

CHAPTER NINE

PHEMIE knew the only way she'd manage to get through the next few days was to focus on work. Thankfully, being at a medical conference, she was able to do just that. Discussing techniques with other doctors during lunch, looking at trade demonstrations and new products on the market, wishing the RFDS had unlimited funds to buy most of the new products. She filled her time with all those things but mostly she was one hundred per cent aware of avoiding Gil at all costs.

It wasn't hard, given she felt he was doing the same thing and as keynote speaker all of his time was scheduled down to the last second. If they had happened to be in the same place at the same time, they ignored the gravitational pull that existed between them and instead focused on niceties. He would ask how her nerves were holding up and she would praise him on his latest speech. He treated her the same way he treated all other delegates—

with polite enthusiasm—and part of her was a little miffed at that reaction.

She *wasn't* the same as everyone else. She was the woman he'd kissed so tenderly and yet was treating like she was…just another person. Phemie knew her reaction was ludicrous. Of course Gil, professional that he was, wouldn't treat her any differently in front of other delegates simply because there might be the far-off possibility that he had an emotional attachment to her.

If he'd walked in, hauled her into his arms then dipped her backwards before planting a big smoochy kiss on her mouth, well…Phemie's breathing increased just thinking about it. She closed her eyes and worked at controlling herself before focussing on what was happening up on the podium.

It would be her turn soon. After the next break, she would be required to take the lead and present her work to the entire conference. Mentally she ran through her presentation again, hoping beyond hope that her computer didn't falter, that the laser pointer would work, that there wouldn't be a blackout.

Her anxiety rising, she quietly slipped out the side door of the convention room and dragged in a deep breath. She needed some air. Fresh air.

Sure steps took her towards the nearest balcony

and within a minute she was breathing in the crisp yet polluted Sydney air. It had been raining but instead of the fresh, cleanness outback rain brought, here in the city the May shower had brought a certain mustiness. It didn't matter. Phemie gripped the edge of the balcony railing and closed her eyes, wishing she could breathe the fresh outback air. She was a long way from home and she knew it. Still, it wouldn't be long until she returned, back to the wide open spaces and her calm, contented life.

Gil would be coming back with her. She'd managed to arrange it all quite easily and now everything was settled. He would be there. With her. At her place. She knew that. Accepted it as fact. It was only for one week. She could cope. Then he would leave and she would put him from her mind and get on with what she did best—helping other people. He would be on the other side of the world and he would no doubt forget— No. She shouldn't be thinking of Gil right now. She focused hard, doing some mental gymnastics to get her mind back in order again.

'Phemie?'

She jumped almost sky high as she spun around, slipping on the slight wetness underfoot but managing to right herself almost immediately. Gil was by her side in an instant, his arms outstretched to her.

'Are you all right? I'm sorry. I didn't mean to startle you.'

'I'm fine.' She took a step away from him, needing the distance. 'What are you doing out here? You should be inside, listening to...' She stopped and shook her head. 'You know what? Do whatever you want. I need to go in now.' She stepped away, making sure her footing was sure and steadfast, given she wasn't used to wearing high-heeled shoes.

'Phemie. Wait.'

She turned and looked at him expectantly.

'Are you angry with me?'

'Angry? Why would I be angry?' There was veiled sarcasm in her tone. 'You say you're my friend, you kiss me and then you brush it aside as though it never happened.'

'I've been a little—'

'Busy. I know. It's fine. Listen, I need to go and calm myself down before my presentation.' Another step towards the door but this time he moved like lightning and was there before her, holding the door open.

'I didn't mean to add to your nervousness. I had to take a call so was already out of the convention room when I saw you leave. I simply wanted to ensure you were feeling all right. With regard to the matter of the other evening...' He paused and exhaled harshly, as though he was cross, but she got the feeling he was more cross with himself than with her. 'I would like to apologise if I've hurt or confused you in any way. That was never my intention.'

'It's fine, Gil. Really.' She walked back into the warmth of the convention centre.

'William tells me we're all set to go on Wednesday.'

'William's coming with you?' She was surprised at this news.

'No. By "we" I meant us.'

'Right. Yes. It's all been cleared for you to come back to the Didja base with me.' She made sure her words were calm, controlled and concise, not wanting to tell him how her boss had gushed at the thought of having such a prestigious doctor taking an interest in the RFDS. Gil's ego had been stroked more than enough during the conference. He didn't need more. 'We'll meet nice and early in the lobby. I think the flight is booked for six am. It'll be a long day of travelling so don't party too much.'

'I won't. I assure you.' His smile was equally as polite and Phemie nodded before turning away from him again. 'Uh…just one more thing.'

She turned, trying to remain calm. So much for getting her thoughts into gear. So much for focusing on the task at hand. All she was conscious of was Gil's light, spicy cologne, the warmth emanating from his gorgeous body and the way he made her knees turn to jelly when he looked at her the way he was doing right now.

'You'll do absolutely fine with your presentation.'

'How do you know? You haven't heard it.'

'I just know. Trust me on that and to combat the nerves, just do what I do.'

'What? Picture the audience in their underwear?'

'Heavens, no.' He gave a nervous chuckle at that idea. If he'd pictured Phemie in her underwear when he'd been speaking at the podium, he'd more than likely have had a stroke because she had an incredible body. In fact, he had to school his thoughts right now from picturing her in her underwear. 'Just before I'm about to stand up to speak, I bite my tongue, blink five times, squeeze my little fingers and snort.'

Phemie looked at him with utter incredulity before bursting out laughing. 'Do you really?'

'No, but having someone make me laugh does help. Usually I call on William but during the past year I've heard all his jokes and, believe me, they weren't that good to start with.'

Phemie's smile was bright and natural and Gil hadn't realised just how much he'd missed seeing it.

'Dr Grainger?' One of the conference organisers came over. 'We'll be ready for you soon. If you'd like to get your things and come this way?'

'OK.' Phemie took a few steps away but looked at Gil over her shoulder. 'Thanks.'

'You're welcome.' His smile was natural and gorgeous and she felt her knees starting to wobble again. 'Break a leg.'

'I guess you can feel quite safe saying that at a medical conference, but here in Australia we say "Chookas" instead.'

'Really?' The look he gave her said he wasn't sure whether or not she was pulling his leg. 'Well...in that case, er...chookas, Dr Grainger.' The smile on her face made her eyes sparkle and Gil felt the full effect, recalling just how intoxicating those lips of hers really were.

'Thank you, Professor.' As she turned and walked away, Phemie couldn't believe how much brighter she felt. Her nerves had all but disappeared and she was more than ready to stand in front of the delegates and give her presentation. And it was all thanks to Gil.

Phemie didn't see him again until Wednesday morning when they met in the hotel lobby before the sun had started to rise, in readiness for travelling to the airport to begin their journey to Didja.

'Good morning, Euphemia.' Gil greeted her with cheery politeness.

'How many cups of tea have you already had?' she asked, slumping down in the chair and pulling a face at his overly bright attitude.

'Only two cups of what you term "dishwater" this morning.'

Phemie sighed, a small smile touching her lips. 'Well, I've had no tea and no coffee either, so please stop being all sunshiny.'

Gil's lips twitched. 'Not a morning person, then?'

'More like a "don't disturb my sleep" sort of person.'

'Yet you're a doctor. That's a profession guaranteed to have high sleep deprivation.'

'Yet it rarely happens that we get called out to emergencies in the wee small hours of the morning.' She let her eyes drift shut but was more than aware of every move, every breath Gil took. How could she be so in tune with him? She'd known him for less than a week and this was the reaction she was having towards him. Imagine what she'd be like after the coming week in the outback…alone…together!

'You were the one who set the flight times,' he pointed out with complete logic. 'I'm sure we could have taken a later flight, thus giving you time to sleep.'

She opened her eyes. 'Actually, the morning flights are the only ones that go direct between the state capital cities. Other than that, we would have been flying from Sydney to Melbourne then to Adelaide then to Perth, where we would switch to the smaller aircraft to fly from Perth to Kalgoorlie and then drive to the base. The trip would have been completed when the sun had already set and as you mentioned that you don't necessarily like to fly…' She trailed off.

'Yes. Yes. I accept the early hour.' Gil shook his head, trying to remain positive in light of hearing her outline their travel plans. He knew it was going to be a long day, most of it spent in the confines of a plane, but for some reason, having Phemie Grainger sitting beside him was definitely taking the edge off the loathing he felt for flying.

Phemie yawned and closed her eyes. 'As it's going to be a long day's travelling, the sooner it's over, the better.' She sighed and relaxed further into the softness of the chair.

Gil watched her for a moment before calling over a hotel staff member. He spoke in hushed tones and then returned his full attention to the tired yet highly alluring woman before him. 'You don't like to travel?'

Phemie opened an eye for a second then closed it. 'Oh, I like travelling. I just prefer doing it to my own schedule. If the planes would run at exactly the times I wanted, I'd be more than happy. Perhaps even chipper.'

'You're a planner, eh?'

'A meticulous planner. My mother used to call me...' she yawned again, her eyes barely open '...Miss Hospital Corners when I was growing up.'

'Fairly apt, now, given you're a doctor.'

'That's what she thinks.' Phemie sat there, allowing her body a few more seconds of sleep. 'Oh.' She sat bolt upright and stared at Gil. 'Was I supposed to organise a taxi or have you alr—?'

'It's been taken care of.'

Phemie relaxed back in the chair again. 'Thank you.'

'Ah. Here we are,' Gil said, and this time Phemie really opened her eyes, smelling the delicious aroma of freshly brewed coffee. He waved his hands in a flourish. 'Ta-dah. This should help you.'

'Coffee?'

'Croissants and fruit, too,' he pointed out with a smile.

'Where? How?' Phemie watched as two staff members set the small coffee table between the lounge chairs with the food and drink Gil had somehow ordered.

'Here.' He poured her a cup of coffee. 'Milk? Sugar?'

'Black is fine.' She held out her hand and eagerly accepted his offering. 'Thank you. That was very thoughtful.' Why did he have to be that way? It only made him more endearing.

His gaze encompassed Phemie, his tone intimate and soft as he watched her sip the dark liquid. 'But remember, if you get sleepy today, feel free to rest your head on my shoulder.'

Phemie was pleased and surprised by his words. 'Uh…I'll keep that in mind.' Even the thought of doing that brought warmth to her body and a pale pink tinge to her cheeks.

'I hope you do.' There was a deep promise behind his eyes and it was one that told her he thought of her as more than just a friend. Yes, he'd declared they were friends and she'd agreed, but both of them were kidding themselves if they thought that's all it was between them. Still, for now, for the moment, friendship was good. She didn't need to run from him if it was just friendship, she didn't need to keep her guard up if it was just friendship, she didn't need to constantly be justifying her emotions to herself if it was just friendship.

Years ago, when she'd still dreamed of one day getting married and having children of her own, she had decided that her children would be the best of friends and the best of enemies. They would argue and laugh together. They would share and squabble. They would be normal siblings and she would be their loving mother who ensured they worked out all their differences so they could remain friends throughout adulthood.

She had no idea whether Gil had brothers or sisters and that just highlighted how little she really knew this man who was constantly in her thoughts. Seeing him with Anthony, how he'd treated her brother with respect and friendliness, had improved her opinion of him. Seeing him at the conference and the way he'd neatly fielded questions, spoken with enthusiasm and had given even the lowest in the medical hierarchy his undivided attention had improved her respect for him. Seeing how he was so thoughtful where she was concerned had improved her love for him.

Love!

Her eyes bugged wide open at that and she must have made a little sound as Gil immediately turned to look at her.

'Phemie? Are you all right?'

'Uh…' She looked away and swallowed. 'I'm fine.' She forced a smile. 'Coffee's still a little hot. Burnt my tongue,' she lied, whilst her mind completely rejected her previous thoughts. Love? No. She wasn't that insane. It would be ridiculous to fall in love with a man she barely knew who lived on the other side of the world…especially when falling in love wasn't in her plan. Not at all.

'Car's here,' Gil announced, and Phemie came back to earth with a thud, surprised to find her coffee finished and her plate empty. She looked at Gil to find him watching her.

'Are you sure you're feeling all right?' he asked again.

'Fine.' She smiled as though to prove it and stood, picking up her luggage.

'I can carry that,' he offered, reaching out for her suitcase, but she shook her head.

'I can manage. Besides, it's on wheels so it's no big drama.' She headed out the hotel's sliding glass doors and stopped short when she reached the kerb. 'A limousine?' Phemie looked quizzically at Gil. 'Is this…is this for us?'

'I thought it might be nice to travel to the airport in a bit of style and luxury,' Gil remarked as their luggage was loaded into the boot.

'I've never been in a limo before.'

'Really? Great. Then I'm glad I booked one.' When Phemie met his gaze, Gil shrugged. 'I thought you deserved a reward after your brilliant presentation. You were by far the best presenter at the conference.'

'Oh. Uh. Thanks.' Phemie felt self-conscious at his words as they climbed into the limo.

'Now,' Gil said, relaxing back, 'William has told me that I'd better not get bitten by any drop bears or hoop snakes. Oh, and I need to remember to check under the toilet seat for red-back spiders.'

Phemie laughed at Gil's words.

'What's so funny?' he asked.

'Who told William about drop bears and hoop snakes?' The smile lit her eyes and Gil tried not to stare too much. She was so incredibly beautiful.

'James Crosby. He's a colleague who lives here in Sydney. Why? Was he wrong?'

'Let's see…drop bears, aka killer koalas, drop from eucalyptus trees and attack you and, uh…hoop snakes bite their tails and then roll down the hill like a hula hoop before slithering over to bite you.'

'So it's true?'

'No. It's all…well, how should I put this…? Er…fictitious.'

Gil's eyebrows hit his hairline. 'Really?' Then he laughed. 'Wait until I tell William he was being teased. He thought Crosby was serious.' Gil paused. 'What about those red-back spiders?'

Phemie nodded, her expression serious. 'Oh, they're very real. Along with the brown snakes and the funnel web spiders.'

'Great. This country sure sounds like an adventure!' Gil eased back into the plush seats.

'Thank you for the limo ride,' Phemie said as she rubbed her hand back and forth over the cream-coloured upholstery. There were little lights in the roof and a fully stocked bar. 'It's fantastic. Anthony's been in a limo before and he took pictures but this…this is…' She looked at Gil, her eyes alive with pleasure. 'It was a lovely gesture.'

'I'm pleased you're enjoying it. It's also a way of thanking you for allowing me to come and stay at your base. I do appreciate everything you've done, the strings you've pulled to organise this, Phemie.'

'It wasn't difficult, Gil. Your name opens a lot of doors in the medical world.'

'At least it works somewhere,' he returned with a smile. It appeared that both of them were on their best behaviour today. After all, they would be spending a lot of time together as they travelled across the country.

Throughout the day, they talked on many topics, Gil even allowing her to read a rough draft of his next article. She was both honoured and flattered as well as being secretly delighted when he'd taken her constructive suggestions seriously.

Whilst they flew, she saw no outward signs of nervousness or anxiety on Gil's part except the way he talked non-stop during take-off and landing. She listened, she absorbed and she relaxed in his company. They were two friends, travelling together. That was all. Her earlier thought about being in love with him was obviously as ludicrous now as it had been when it had first popped into her head. She liked Gil. She admired him. Nothing more than friendship. That was how it had to be.

In Perth, they switched planes and boarded a small Cessna bound for Kalgoorlie. When they arrived in the large outback city, Phemie declared them to be in luck.

'I thought we'd have to drive from here to the base but look.' She pointed out across the two landing strips to where an RFDS plane stood. 'We can hitch a ride with Sardi.'

'Sardi's the pilot, correct?'

'Yes. Good memory.' When Phemie saw her friend again, the two hugged as a way of saying hello. 'I feel as though I've been gone for a year rather than a week,' she murmured as they boarded the aircraft. She watched Gil as he entered the even smaller space and sat in the seat she indicated. Once she was seated, she looked over at him.

'How are you doing?'

'Fine.'

'Liar.'

He turned and smiled at her. 'I'm sure Sardi's a

most competent pilot and I also trust that you would never, knowingly, put me in danger.'

'No. I wouldn't.' He had faith in her. He trusted her. He accepted her. Phemie was overwhelmed at that and reached out to take his hand in hers, linking their fingers together. 'Not too much longer now.'

Gil looked at their entwined hands then back to gaze into her perfect blue eyes. The fact that she had been the one to initiate the contact spoke volumes and the elation he felt overshadowed his tension at flying.

He looked again at their hands, loving the feel of her smooth, soft skin against his. He'd only known her for a week. He'd held her in his arms, he'd talked to her, they'd worked together, he'd been immensely impressed with her on the medical front, he'd watched the way she'd cared for her brother…and not seventy-two hours ago he'd had his mouth pressed to hers in a most engaging and electrifying kiss.

She'd been a constant visitor to his dreams and when he was with her like this, the way her bright cheerful scent enveloped him only made him want to hold her, to be with her, to kiss her again and again. To say he'd reconnected with the world, that he'd been catapulted out of his comfort zone was almost an understatement. Throughout the entire tour he'd slowly withdrawn from his cave, meeting people, chatting, being sociable. He'd realised he *had* missed being connected with the world and whilst he knew he had to return to England, to the life he'd had before, he'd also been ready to stop moving from one hotel to the other. June and Caitie would always be a part of him, he knew that and felt that, but it was indeed time he moved on.

Then he'd met Phemie and she'd turned that level of 'normal' he'd thought he'd found upside down and inside out. She'd brought sunshine into places of his life he hadn't realised were dull and grey. She'd made him re-evaluate what he thought he knew. She'd accepted him as a person, a man in his own right as well as respecting him as a professional. She'd opened his heart and awakened a passion which was addictive. He rubbed his thumb along her finger, relishing in the fact she'd given him permission to touch her, to be with her. The main problem was, he wanted more.

He swallowed the thought. They had a whole week together. Working alongside each other. Talking, having the ability to spend real time alone. He was looking forward to it and decided right there and then that he wasn't going to waste it. Life was for living. He hadn't been doing much of it prior to the fellowship and that meant he had lost ground to make up.

He tightened his grip on her fingers just for a moment and smiled. 'I'm glad you insisted we take the red-eye out of Sydney.'

'It has been a long day.' Why did her tone sound so husky? So intimate? She looked over at him and swallowed, her tongue coming out to wet her lips.

'But a good day.'

A small, inviting smile touched her lips as the tension between them continued to increase. 'Yes.' Phemie nodded and settled back in her seat, the heat from his hand suffusing her body, and she wanted, just this once, to enjoy the effect he had on her.

'So it was worth having your sleep disturbed?'

She looked at him with hooded eyes, trying not to subconsciously beg him to hurry up and press his mouth to hers. 'Indubitably.'

He smiled. 'You are so lovely,' he whispered as he caressed her cheek with his free hand and watched as her eyelids fluttered closed. Her breathing increased and then caught in a gasp when he rubbed his thumb over her lips.

'Gil.'

He heard the veiled hint of pleading and knew what he must do, what they both so desperately wanted. Cupping her chin, he lifted her head and in the next second had his mouth on hers.

Together, they leaned into the kiss, absorbing everything the other had to give, needing to feel, to recapture and expand on what they'd felt last time.

'This is insane,' she murmured against his mouth.

'I know but I can't help myself. You are so totally addictive.'

'We shouldn't be doing this.'

'Why not?'

'Because you live… And I…' Rational thought left her as he once more took her to heights she hadn't thought possible. Her breathing was erratic. His lips were tender and slow.

'We have all week to figure it out.' He spoke softly, desire in his tone.

'Fasten seat belts,' Sardi announced. The pilot's words were enough to bring them both back to reality. Phemie sat up straight and tried to pull her hand free from Gil's but found she couldn't. When she looked at him, his eyes were serious.

'I can't hide what I feel for you, Phemie, but I do want to understand it. To do that, we must do some research.' He kissed her again as the plane started to dip. 'And I have a feeling this is research we'll both enjoy.'

Pandora's Box was now definitely open wide and surprisingly he couldn't wait.

CHAPTER TEN

WHEN Gil had looked down through the window of the small plane to the land below, all he'd seen was what appeared to be a tin shed and two houses.

'That's it?' He was astounded. For some reason when Phemie had said the middle of nowhere, he'd thought she was joking.

'Home, sweet home,' she'd sighed.

'You don't live here, do you?'

'Of course I do.'

'I thought this was just where you worked.'

'It is. The house has sleeping quarters at the rear and the base office at the front.' She pointed. Now that they were getting closer the tin shed appeared much larger and he realised it was a hangar. The houses also came into focus and he realised there was only one official house. The other building was a very large garage where a number of cars were already parked.

She'd continued to hold his hand until Sardi

landed the plane and then, almost reluctantly, had let go but only because she'd needed to open the doors. They retrieved their luggage and walked the short distance to Phemie's home.

'This will be your room,' she murmured, her body still tingling from the kisses. This time Gil hadn't pulled away, hadn't tried to keep his distance as he had the last time he'd pressed his mouth to hers. No, this time he seemed more than happy to continue what they'd both been fighting for the past week.

Phemie opened a door to show him a very basic room. A bed, a table and chair, a lamp, a small wardrobe, a clock and two framed pictures of Australian animals on the walls. That was it. The floor was polished wooden boards and a ceiling fan hung over the bed.

She'd already given Gil a tour of the front part of the house, which was where the RFDS office was situated. Ben had been diligently manning the UHF radio as well as the phones and had been very pleased to meet Professor Gilbert Fitzwilliam.

'Pheme's always reading your articles to me. Pointing things out. Personally, I think she's a little obsessed with you but there are worse things to obsess about, am I right? Besides, she thinks you're a total legend.'

Phemie had stared appalled at her colleague, unable to believe he'd said such embarrassing things. What must Gil think of her? That she was some gushing fan? Well, in a way she was but that had been before she'd come to know him on a more...intimate level. Now, to have Ben say she was obsessed with Gil only made things worse.

When Gil had looked at her, however, she'd quickly pasted on an over-bright smile and ignored the raised eyebrow that indicated he was very interested in what Ben was saying. Mortification still passed through her at the memory and she'd quickly moved Gil away from Ben, leading him to the bedrooms at the rear of the house.

'Sorry it's so basic. I had Ben air it out and remove the boxes I was storing in here. Apparently, he's even made the bed and put out some towels for you.' She pointed to the linen and felt like a right royal twit. Of course Gil could see the towels on the bed. She was nervous. That's all it was and she was starting to babble.

'I must remember to thank him,' Gil murmured, and then looked sheepish. 'I guess I didn't need to say that out loud. I'm used to saying things like that, having William make a note of it and then reminding me to do it later.' He put his suitcase down and took off his hat, waving it to create a small breeze around his face. 'Force of habit.'

'You're a busy man. You can't be expected to remember everything.'

'Yes, but here I'm not Professor Gilbert Fitzwilliam, Emergency Medicine Specialist Travelling Fellowship.'

'No. You're just…Gil.'

A broad smile crossed his face and his eyes lit with delight. Phemie tried not to be affected but still put a hand on the doorjamb for support. 'I like the sound of that. Just…Gil. I don't think I've been just Gil for quite some time.'

Why did the man have to be so incredibly good-looking? Why did he have to be here in her home? So close yet so far. The two of them all alone. She looked away and focused on a very interesting knot of wood in the floor boards.

'It's going to be great here. I can feel it now.' He walked further into the room and looked around. For all its sparseness, it was clean. The other reason he'd moved was because he needed to distance himself from Phemie. She was an incredible woman and one he was having a difficult time ignoring. The need to scoop her into his arms and carry her to bed was overwhelmingly powerful and he knew he needed to resist. At least, for now.

Gil smiled and the look in her eyes told him she was as aware of him as he was of her. A spark of desire had flared briefly behind her gorgeous blue eyes before she'd started studying the floor.

It appeared he wasn't the only one who was a little uncertain about the two of them being here alone and she had raised a good point on the plane. They lived on opposite sides of the globe. However, he did believe that during this week they'd find some way to work things out because what he felt for her was something that could no longer be ignored.

'Uh…' Phemie pointed up at the ceiling. 'Fan. A must in the outback.' She tapped the switch on the wall. 'Not rocket science. One is fast. Five is slow. The window.' She pointed. 'Try and ensure the screens are closed at all times. You may want to sleep with the window open, though. We get a nice breeze sweeping through most nights. Gives a bit of respite from the heat.'

'Pleased to hear that.' He walked over to where she stood and switched on the ceiling fan, its gentle whir the only sound in the room apart from their breathing. He was standing close to her and he could tell she was trying to resist the urge to take a step backwards, to put distance between them. 'Ahh…that should help cool me down.'

There was a thickness to his words that made Phemie wonder whether he was referring to the heat outside, which had hit them like a ten-tonne truck the instant they'd embarked from the aircraft, or the fact that they were in close proximity to each other.

She started to perspire, her body heat definitely continuing to rise, and as *she* was more accustomed to the dry heat, it had to be Gil's nearness causing the reaction. What she needed was a cold shower, rather than the breeze from the ceiling fan. Swallowing, she forced her legs to work, to move her away from him before she succumbed to the temptation to lean forward and press her mouth to his. He really was becoming utterly addictive.

'Bathroom.' The word came out as a breathless whisper and she quickly cleared her throat as she stepped into the hallway, her flat-heeled boots sounding on the floorboards. 'Bathroom is just opposite here. We'll be, uh…sharing the amenities…' again she couldn't meet his gaze '…so knocking whenever the doors are shut should be a good way to ensure we don't, uh…walk in on…each other.'

Her breathing continued its erratic increase and she realised she was behaving like a schoolgirl, aroused simply by thinking of Gil naked in the shower, that solid and firm body of his glistening with drops of water. Stop it! She shook her head and took a quick deep breath, hoping to get herself back under control.

'We're also under strict water restrictions so all showers are a matter of wetting yourself down, turning off the water, soaping, then turning the taps back on for rinsing and so on. On and off with the taps is the way to go. Every drop is precious. Uh…toilet is a septic tank so if it gets blocked, you'll be the one clearing it.'

'Fair enough.' There was a tinge of humour in his words and Phemie glanced up, her eyes now blazing with annoyance. She was trying so hard to control herself and obviously he found it amusing! 'This isn't a joking matter, Gil. Water is a precious and very valuable commodity out here. We're on tank water, which means it really only gets filled up when it rains. As it rarely rains, we have to use what we have sparingly.

He sobered instantly. 'Agreed, and I wasn't joking about the water.'

'You were. You smiled when I mentioned the restrictions,' she remarked accusingly.

'No. I was amused at the way you were explaining about the septic tank. You blushed when you talked about a blocked toilet. I thought that was adorable.'

Phemie's annoyance disappeared instantly. 'Adorable?' She looked into his eyes and he immediately moved closer. 'Don't, Gil.' She put her hand up to stop him but it collided with his chest. He quickly covered her hand, holding it against his heart.

'This thing between us is only intensifying with every passing moment, Euphemia.' His words were soft, warm and filled with truth as he slipped his other hand around her waist. 'As I said before, we have a week to do some research, to figure out what this attraction really means.'

'Gil. It doesn't matter. I can't.'

'Can't what? Do you have any idea what it means for me to feel this way about you?' His words were soft, entrancing. 'These types of emotions don't come along every day. This isn't any ordinary attraction, Phemie. It's powerful and it's *real*.'

'I understand but I...' She trailed off as he brushed a kiss first to one cheek then the other, her eyelids fluttering closed as she relished the contact.

'I've been in a relationship, I've been married, I've loved and lost and I've been so incredibly alone. This fellowship has forced me to reconnect with the world but you've helped me to reconnect with my heart.'

Phemie was a little puzzled and swallowed over the dryness in her throat. 'What are you saying? That you l...?' She broke off, not sure she wanted to know the answer to that question.

'Like you?' Gil finished for her, and she opened her eyes to look into his mesmerising brown depths. 'Yes. I like you *a lot*.' The question remained as to what she felt for him. Was it lust? Was it like? Was it more?

'Everything's happening so fast,' she whispered. 'I'm not the marrying kind, Gil.'

He raised an eyebrow at that. 'A modern girl? Preferring to live together?' He was definitely surprised.

'No.' She shook her head. 'It's not that.' She dragged strength from somewhere deep down inside and forced herself to push away from him, to put distance between them both emotionally and physically.

'I'm confused.'

'I'm not the marrying kind, Gil, because I plan never to marry.'

'Not ever?' he asked with incredulity.

'Not ever,' she confirmed, and with that she turned on her heel and walked away from him, leaving him stunned.

Ten minutes later Ben, the RFDS administrator, came to look for him.

'Problem?' Gil asked as he looked up from the desk in his room where he'd been engrossed in some articles. He'd had a quick wash and changed his clothes yet after Phemie had dropped such a bomb-shell, especially since he'd confessed his interest in her, he'd retreated back into his work, needing to pull himself together in order to face her again.

'Callout. You right to go?' Ben asked, but Gil was already on his feet, reaching for his hat and sunglasses.

'Lead the way.' As he followed Ben to the front of the house, he found Phemie on the UHF radio.

'Is Rajene there, over?' she asked.

'Dad's gone to get her now, over,' a young man's voice replied.

'OK, Peter. We'll be there as soon as we can, over and out.' Phemie put the handset down and turned to face Gil, hoping her knees would continue to support her because when he was around, she often had trouble standing.

'What's happening?' Gil asked.

'Gemma Etherington's about to have her baby. We need to provide medical support until Sardi can pick up Melissa and Iris from the Didja clinic.'

'Melissa and Iris are…?' Gil waited.

'Melissa's an OB/GYN and Iris, Dex's fiancée, is a paediatrician.'

'Of course. I do recall him mentioning her now.' Gil nodded and Phemie was pleased to see he was in full professional mode. 'Where do we begin?'

'I'm going to quickly make a Thermos of coffee for me, tea for you, change my clothes, pack my medical bag and then we'll be ready to go.'

'So there's no rushing out the door in a wild flurry of excitement?'

Phemie couldn't help but smile as she headed into the kitchen. She filled the kettle from the water cooler before switching it on, knowing without turning around that Gil had followed her.

Her ability to sense his presence was becoming acute. 'You've been watching too many movies, Professor. Whilst Sardi keeps the plane checked and ready to go, there are still a few last-minute flight details she needs to go over so we have about five to ten minutes before we'll be in the air.'

'Right. Good.' He pointed towards the bed-rooms. 'You go change. I can make the drinks.'

'It's OK. I can do—'

'I'm here to help, remember.' He pinned her with a glare, his words calm. 'So let me help.'

Phemie shrugged and decided it was easier to retreat than argue.

'Pheme?' Ben called out. 'Will you be needing Madge at all? She's about twenty minutes away from the Etheringtons', having been out at the Prices', doing an immunisation clinic with Dex today.'

'I don't think so,' she called back. 'With Gil along, plus Rajene and knowing Melissa and Iris will be on their way, I think we'll have more help then we can poke a stick at.'

'Righto. Sardi will be ready in five,' Ben replied.

'Go.' Gil pointed in the direction of the bedrooms. Phemie did as she was told and when she returned, it was to find the drinks made and her medical bag packed. Gil and Ben were discussing the case.

'She already has six children?' Gil's eyes almost bugged out of his head at Ben's words.

'This is number seven,' Phemie added as she peered into the bag, quickly checking things through. 'Right, Gil. Grab the drinks and let's go.'

They headed out to the airstrip, where Sardi was in the cockpit going through her final checks. 'Back so soon?' she joked as they boarded. Phemie went through the routine of pulling up the steps and ensuring everything was locked down and secure.

'How are you doing?' she asked Gil.

'I've been better,' he said truthfully, and she didn't miss the different meaning of his words.

As she wasn't yet ready to discuss it any further she said, 'I mean with the flying.'

'I knew exactly what you meant, Euphemia. I chose to misinterpret. I'm fine with the flying. Thank you for your concern.' He was brisk and polite and she knew she really couldn't expect more. He'd all but laid himself on the line, telling her he was interested in her, and she'd pushed him away. It wasn't that she *wasn't* interested in him— quite the contrary—and that was the main problem. She *wanted* to see where this attraction might lead but if it lead anywhere towards marriage, towards children then she would end up hurting them both. No. She'd made her decision years ago and whilst the fleeting thought that she was already in the process of falling in love with Gil had passed through her mind, not acting on those emotions would no doubt save them both in the end. It was better that by the end of his week here that they part as friends, rather than enemies.

Phemie sat down and clipped herself into her seat. Moments later, they were in the air and when she looked across at Gil, it was to find him peering out the window. 'I'm sorry, Gil.'

'About?'

'What I said before. It was bad timing and I didn't mean any offence.'

'Is it true?'

'That I don't want to marry? Yes.'

'Then don't be sorry. At least you're honest. A man can't help but admire honesty in a woman even if she's saying things he doesn't want to hear.' He turned and continued to stare out the window.

Phemie tried to take his words at face value but her mind was in a whirl. Was he just saying that to be nice? As he'd been married once and it had ended in pain, she'd been quite surprised when he'd intimated marriage earlier on. Was that what he really wanted? Did he really plan to marry again? If he was willing to take such a risk again, surely that should indicate his feelings for her were indeed growing stronger with each passing day.

But what about the distance factor? They lived on opposite sides of the world. How could they possibly get married, or even begin to think along such lines when there was the huge obstacle of geographical location to consider?

It was probably just as well she'd admitted the truth to him. Telling him she planned never to marry was the right thing to do and now they could go back to their own lives at the end of this week, him in his country, she in hers.

It couldn't matter that she thought him the best man in the world. It couldn't matter that she wanted him to hold her hand, to be near her, to kiss her for the rest of her days. It couldn't matter that she had fallen in love with him because if she *did* let it matter, she would disappoint him in so many different ways. It simply wouldn't be fair to commit to a relationship, to marriage with Gil when she knew there was a risk of having a Down's syndrome child.

Then again, Gil had been wonderful with Anthony. He seemed to accept people for who they were, from whatever walks of life they had come. What would happen if they *did* get married, if they *did* have children and if one of those kids *had* Down's? She glanced over at Gil who was still peering out the window, excitement etched on his features. How would he react? She presumed, from what she knew of him, that he would embrace that child—any children they had—with the utmost love and conviction. When she thought of it like that, it certainly made a very appealing picture.

Gil was definitely challenging her, making her think of how different things could be. She'd always thought it would be safer not to risk having children, not to risk passing on the TT21 gene, but even the fact that she was now thinking about the possibility of an alternative life from the one she'd mapped out for herself illustrated just how much Gil was influencing her life.

For now, though, Phemie decided it was best to leave any other attempts at conversation and instead focused her mind on Gemma Etherington's possible needs.

When they were close to landing, Phemie ran through what would happen next so Gil wasn't floundering. 'As soon as we land, we'll be driven by ute to the homestead and then the real fun begins.'

'I completely comprehend the situation as it pertains to the medical emergency but I have to confess it's quite thrilling to be *flying* to someone's house to help them out.' He shook his head in wonderment. 'England is so small. Australia is so vast.' There was excitement in his tone and Phemie couldn't help but smile, pleased he seemed to have let go of their previous conversation. She knew it was by no means over but for now it was as though a medical truce had been called. They needed to be able to rely upon each other for the sake of their patient.

'I know how you feel.'

'You do?' He seemed surprised.

'Of course. We've all felt exactly the same way when we head off on our first call with the RFDS. Flying to a patient's home is different from driving there or having them come to you. It does become second nature to you after a while because it's a part of your everyday life. Although having you here, with your exuberance, helps us all to rekindle the love of what it is we do.'

'Good.' Gil nodded. 'Glad to be of help even before we've hit the ground.'

'Right…well, as Ben mentioned, Gemma's having her seventh child but back in January when she was about twenty weeks, she had a few problems. There were a few ante-partum bleeds but Melissa managed to sort everything out. Gemma, however, was put on complete bed rest for the duration of her pregnancy. Rajene, who's a retired midwife from Tarparnii, lives next door and has been performing daily checks on Gemma and the baby, giving the necessary steroid injections and any other treatments Melissa's prescribed.'

'A Tarparniian midwife, eh?' Gil was clearly impressed. 'I'm looking forward to meeting Rajene.'

'Of course. I keep forgetting you worked in Tarparnii and with Dex, no less.'

'You are correct. I went there not long after the death of my family.'

'Your *family*?' Phemie was stunned. 'You didn't say…' She stopped and waved away her words. 'I'm sorry, Gil. It's none of my—'

'Business?' He finished for her, his eyes dark and cloudy as he spoke. 'When I told you the other night that my wife had died in a plane crash, I left out the other detail, the one which still grips my heart every time I bring it up.'

'Gil. You don't have to—'

He held up his hand to stop her. 'I want you to know, Euphemia. With the way my feelings for you are intensifying, you have a right to know.'

'Gil—'

'Shh. You see, June, my wife, was travelling home, having taken our eight-month-old baby girl to see her family in Italy. My Caitie, my beautiful Caitie. June was holding her on her lap…' The rest of his sentence hung in the air and with both of them being emergency medicine specialists, they knew all too well the circumstances that would have followed.

'Oh, Gil.' Immediately, she reached across and took his hand in hers, her eyes filled with love. Her heart churned with the pain he must have felt, how he would have thought his world had been destroyed, how he would have questioned everything over and over again. Why? Why had it happened? Why had his family been taken from him? She'd heard before, from close friends, that it was possible, when you were really close, really connected with someone special, that you could feel their pain as though it were your own. That was how Phemie felt now, as though it was *her* pain, *her* family, *her* utter devastation. So strong was the bond she'd somehow forged with this man that she was deeply affected.

'How soul-destroying.'

Gil was overwhelmed at her response and put his hand over hers. He'd received sad looks, pitying looks, sympathy from everyone he'd worked with. Phemie's open and honest emotions were so very genuine, and he couldn't help but be touched.

'Almost there,' Sardi said, and both Phemie and Gil looked out the window as they flew over the Etheringtons' homestead. Neither of them spoke. Neither of them moved, their hands staying inter-twined until they'd touched down, and even then it felt as though the only reason they were letting go was because they needed to work.

Every time she tried to distance herself from him, something happened to draw her closer again. Not that she hadn't wanted him to share his most soul-destroying past with her. She was honoured he trusted her and it did help her to understand him better. Why he'd locked himself away, why he'd written so many articles, con-ducted such a variety of research projects, why he'd accepted the travelling fellowship. Anything and everything to help him come to terms with what had happened to his family.

His family. Gil had been a father and there was no doubt, given the way he'd tenderly spoken his daughter's name, that he'd loved being a dad. That was another reason why there was absolutely no hope for them as a couple. Even if she entertained the idea that Gil might want her, might want to be with her, even marry her, they could never have children. It was too risky.

Gil's brightness returned as they climbed into Ron Etherington's four-door ute. Phemie decided to follow his example and be bright and happy but that didn't stop his revelation from playing over and over in the back of her mind. She climbed into the back seat, urging him into the front so he could get a close look at the 'outback'. Soon they were bumping over a dusty track, which Ron obviously thought was a well-defined road. Then again, maybe the man was taking a short cut as his wife was in labour.

'I dropped Rajene off at the house about ten minutes ago. I've gotta tell ya, Pheme, I'm mighty glad she lives close by. Gems was starting to pant and said the pains were getting worse every time she had a contraction.'

'Sounds as though things are moving along nicely.'

Ron laughed and took his hand off the wheel for a second. 'Look at me. I'm shaking. It's been like this every single time one of the kids has been born. I turn into a mess but this time…' He sobered a little. 'What with all the problems and everything…'

'Melissa has kept us apprised of Gemma's condition and as she's been taking it easy and resting and generally doing everything she's told, Gemma's given this baby the best chance in the world. Plus, she's carried it almost to term. Thirty-six weeks—that's excellent, Ron.'

'Good. Good. Almost there. Hang in there, my beautiful Gem,' he called with a whoop, even though there was no way his wife could hear him. 'The cavalry is coming.'

The makeshift road was less bumpy now and as Ron rounded a bend, the homestead came into view. It was just as Gil had pictured, having only seen the roof from up above. It was long, slightly raised off the ground and a wide verandah circled the entire building. The epitome of an outback homestead. He loved it.

'When we arrive,' Phemie said, and he angled himself in his seat so he could see her better, 'I'll take point. We stabilise, control the labour and do our best to keep everything and everyone calm until the experts get here.' She patted the medical bags on either side of her. One was the bag Ben had packed and the other was from the plane, containing the heavier equipment such as a portable sphygmomanometer and a portable foetal heart monitor.

'Right. Sounds straightforward.'

'Except that this is Gemma's seventh child and as a rule she should deliver quite quickly. We don't have the usual equipment hospitals have so improvisation is key.'

'Improvise. Right.' Gil nodded. He was serious, he was concentrating but the energetic buzz that emanated from him was almost overpowering. He was really enjoying this. She was about to ask how long it had been since he'd delivered a baby but didn't want to worry Ron in case Gil's answer wasn't what she wanted to hear. She simply hoped that Melissa and Iris would make it in time.

Finally, after what seemed like an eternity since they'd received the call back at the base, Gil and Phemie were rushing through the rear door of the homestead after Ron had practically parked on the back steps.

'They're in the bedroom,' Ron called, leading the way to his wife's side. The scene that met them on entering the room wasn't what Phemie had wanted to see. Gemma was lying on her back, propped up on her elbows, her feet pressed hard against the footboard of their bed. The bed had been stripped of its linen and was covered with a plastic protective sheet. Another protective sheet was on the floor and towels were draped over the polished wood at the base of the bed. Rajene was helping Gemma to breathe through a contraction.

Phemie took the equipment bag from Gil, who'd carried it in, and handed the portable sphygmo to him whilst she set up the foetal heart monitor. 'Gemma and Rajene, this is Gil. He's helping out for the week.'

Gemma, red faced and cheeks puffed, nodded but didn't miss a beat. Rajene gave a polite smile, which broadened when Gil greeted her in her native Tarparnese tongue.

'Report, please?' Phemie asked the midwife.

'She is almost to the full stage of dilatation.'

Phemie had a quick feel of the outside of Gemma's belly whilst Gil checked her blood pressure with the sphygmo. 'Very tight. Let's see what the heartbeat is doing.' The sound of the baby's heartbeat filled the air and brought a tired smile to Gemma's lips and a whoop of elation from Ron's. A second later Gemma braced herself against the foot board and moaned as she pushed.

'What? No. That can't be a push.' Phemie looked stunned.

'It was,' Gemma grunted through clenched teeth.

'But it's going to be another half an hour at least until Melissa and Iris get here.'

'Tell that to the baby,' Gemma remarked.

Phemie pulled on a pair of gloves and did an internal examination. 'You're fully dilated, Gem. I guess this baby's coming now despite knowing the specialists are on their way.'

'How long is it since either of you delivered a baby?' Gemma asked between pants, her question directed at both Phemie and Gil.

'Uh…a while.' It wasn't the fact of delivering a baby that had Phemie on edge but more the fact that Gemma's pregnancy hadn't been easy. What if something went wrong with the birth? What if there was something wrong with the baby? She silently wished for her colleagues—colleagues with years of experience in these matters—to hurry.

'A longer while,' came Gil's reply. He looked at Phemie and she could almost feel him reading her thoughts. If everything ran to course, they'd be fine. It was all the unknown variables that concerned them.

'OK, then. Well, as it's not been that long since

I went through this,' she panted. 'I'll talk you both through each step.'

'No one's doubting your experience but I have to say there's nothing like having the experienced mother to talk the doctors through the procedure. I think I'm going to need to write this experience up in a medical journal otherwise no one will believe me,' Gil murmured, and received a laugh from Gemma.

'I like this one, Phemie. Good-looking and funny. Can we keep him?'

Phemie instantly raised her eyes to meet Gil's and found him watching her with equal intent. Could she? Could she keep him here with her? In the outback? Would he stay? She hadn't even thought of that before. Would he give up his life in England, his prestige and fame to become an outback doctor? If he stayed, though, what would that mean for her?

CHAPTER ELEVEN

WHILST Gemma's pregnancy had endured quite a few ups and downs, it appeared the delivery was going to be straightforward and for that alone Phemie was thankful. It also helped that Rajene, midwife extraordinaire, was there, guiding them in confused English. A few times, though, she would revert to Tarparnese when she couldn't think of the right description in English and Phemie was exceedingly grateful that Gil was there to converse easily with the woman in her native tongue.

'All right, Gemma.' Phemie positioned herself at the bottom of the bed, protective gown over her clothes, gloves on her hands and a prayer in her heart. 'Push when you're ready.'

Gemma grunted and groaned as another contraction hit and, straining against Rajene on one side and Ron on the other, she pushed her hardest.

'The head is crowning,' Phemie announced.

'That was great, Gemma,' she encouraged once the contraction had passed.

Rajene slipped a few pillows behind Gemma so she could rest between contractions and conserve as much energy as possible. Ron spoke words of encouragement and Phemie was peripherally conscious of the Etherington children hovering outside in the hallway. For the older ones, it wasn't the first time they'd seen the birth of one of their siblings. Gemma had delivered the last four of her brood here in this very room. However, Phemie was well aware that Melissa had organised to induce Gemma's pregnancy in two weeks' time to hopefully avoid any delivery and post-partum complications. That, it appeared, was not meant to be.

While waiting for Gemma's next contraction, Gil checked the baby's heartbeat and monitored Gemma's blood pressure. He was also in the process of setting up an area to receive the newborn baby. With confidence, he'd gone through Phemie's medical bag, pulling out what he needed and laying down blankets and freshly laundered towels on a small coffee table, which had been brought in for that purpose.

It was interesting to be sharing this experience

with him—a man she barely knew. It was as though he'd waltzed into her life and changed it for ever.

He made her feel gooey inside and every time he looked at her it was all she could do not to catch her breath and sigh. He was so incredibly handsome, of that there was no doubt. She liked his thick brown hair and, even though he wore it short, she itched to run her fingers through it. She could look into his gorgeous and mesmerising eyes for ever and each time, she knew, they would turn her insides to mush. She wanted to touch his taut, firm body which, as he was now only wearing a polo shirt rather than the usual business shirt, showed off his gorgeous arm muscles.

Phemie remembered all too well what it had been like to have those arms around her, holding her close, keeping her safe. He'd protected her on the train when the emergency brake had been pulled. He'd offered comfort when she'd cried after Mary had left the crash site. He'd tenderly caressed when he'd been showering her with mind-melting kisses.

She felt safe with Gil. She knew he would never intentionally hurt her, just as she would never intentionally hurt him. She knew she could trust him, just as she hoped he found her worthy of that same quality. She not only admired his intellect but the way he used it and she'd felt unworthy of his praise when he'd called her smart.

He may have been through his own personal trauma with the death of his wife and baby but he had gone on with his life. He'd chosen to share his research and experiences with medics around the world and the fact he'd done all this whilst carrying such a personal hurt deep down inside only made her respect him even more.

'Sardi's just called through,' Peter, Gemma and Ron's oldest son, announced from the doorway. 'They've just left Didja.'

Phemie brought her thoughts back into focus as Gemma had another contraction. 'That's it. Push. Push. Keep pushing. The head is almost out. You're doing great.'

When the contraction ended, Gil once more performed the observations. 'Blood pressure is fine. Baby's heartbeat is still strong and healthy.'

Rajene and Ron were adding their words of praise, sponging the very hot and tired Gemma and giving her sips of water. Gil came around and knelt down next to Phemie, the warmth of his body so close it caused her skin to tingle. It was utterly ridiculous the way this man could affect her.

'I'm happy to take care of the baby once it's delivered but what if the baby requires oxygen? I know we brought the oxygen cylinder from the plane and I have a mask to give it to Gemma should she require it, but what about the baby? We don't have a humidicrib or an oxygen tent or any other pieces of equipment.'

Phemie nodded, understanding his concern. She kept her voice low but clear. 'This is outback medicine, Gil. If we don't have what we need, we improvise. You're a highly intelligent man, Professor Fitzwilliam. Think of a way to make what you need.'

As she watched, it was as though she saw his brilliant mind absorb her words and then click into action. He moved to the side of the room as Gemma had another contraction, this one so strong she was able to push the baby's head out.

Phemie knew there was no way Melissa and Iris were going to make it in time. Given that this was Gemma's seventh child, her body knew the cues, when to push, when not to push. Phemie checked to see if the cord was looped around the baby's neck but thankfully there was nothing there.

'The shoulders are rotating so when you're ready, some nice big pushes,' Phemie instructed.

'I thought you didn't know what you were doing?' Gemma quizzed, and Phemie smiled, pleased to see the mother's sense of humour was still intact. 'You're a big liar, Euphemia Graing—' Gemma pushed as the contraction hit.

When she was finished, Phemie looked at her friend. 'I didn't say I didn't know what I was doing. I merely said it had been a while since I'd delivered a baby.'

'Plus with all the problems Gem's had with this pregnancy,' Ron added. 'We don't know what—' He cut himself off and looked out the window, as though wishing the RFDS plane to instantly materialise.

'Whilst I think we'll all be happy when the cavalry arrives, we're all doing extremely well as it is.' Gil's voice was filled with reassurance and strength. 'Especially Gemma.' He smiled at the woman lying on the bed, panting between contractions, and Phemie couldn't believe how in that one instant any worry lines that had been etched on the labouring woman's brow lifted.

Not only was Gil a fantastic medical specialist, a great researcher and an excellent writer, he also had the ability to connect with his patients, to put them at ease and to leave everyone feeling as though everything would, indeed, be all right.

From then on a wave of determination filled the room. Phemie was conscious of Gil going over to speak to Peter, asking him for a few different things. When Peter returned, it was with his arms bundled with Gaffer tape, kitchen plastic wrap and a set of small plastic rods, which usually snapped together to form a platform to dry woollen jumpers.

Phemie wanted to watch whatever it was Gil was up to. She'd told him to improvise and it looked as though he was doing just that. However, Gemma and the baby required her attention and as Gemma continued to push, Phemie guided the small baby into the world.

Ron was there, watching the final moments of the birth, and finally was ready to announce in a loud booming voice that they had another daughter. Gemma laughed and collapsed back against the pillows, Rajene tending to the mother.

Gil had finished whatever it was he'd been doing and was by her side with a warmed towel to accept the newborn, his big hands forming a secure platform. Phemie retrieved two pairs of locking forceps from her bag and clamped the umbilical cord. Then she held out some scissors to Ron.

'Doing the honours, Dad?'

'Try and stop me.' Ron was elated and when it

was done, Phemie looked at the baby, wiping her mouth and nose. A mild cry came out and Gemma sighed with relief.

'She's OK.'

Gil and Phemie waited as the little bundle started breathing, trying to find her rhythm. Phemie quickly administered an injection of vitamin K then frowned as she watched the rise and fall of the little chest more closely. 'Those breaths are a little fast.' When she looked at Gil, she realised he was counting the breaths.

'Ninety,' he said after a minute had passed.

'Rajene.' Phemie looked at the wise midwife. 'Would you mind helping Gemma with the last stage of labour, please?'

'What…what's wrong?' Ron asked, his gaze darting around the room, to his wife on the bed, to his other children in the hallway, to his new little daughter who was being closely watched by the two doctors.

'Peter, check on the plane,' Phemie called. 'If they're close, drive out to the airstrip to meet them.'

'Right.' The seventeen-year-old headed to do as he was told.

'What's going on?' Gemma asked, concern touching her voice.

'The baby's breathing a little too fast, trying to suck in as much air as possible,' Phemie said, taking the baby closer to Gemma. 'See? Her nostrils are flaring and you can see her ribs as her lungs try to work as hard as they can.'

'That's bad?'

'It's an indication of HMD—hyline membrane disease. We need to get her saturations stabilised.'

'Good call,' Gil said as he placed the baby down on the table he'd set up. There were heaters on either side so they could keep the baby warm and finally Phemie was able to see what it was he'd been constructing.

'An oxygen tent.' She shook her head in wonderment. 'Well done.'

'Her skin's pale and mottling.'

'Let's get her hooked up.' With Gil's improvised oxygen tent, they'd be able to apply the oxygen and improve the saturations in no time.

'Yolanda…' Ron was calling to his oldest daughter. 'Call through to the base so they can get a message to the plane that it's HMD.'

'Is she all right?' Gemma asked, her tone watery and scared. Rajene was busy delivering the afterbirth but was keeping a close eye on the mother.

'We're working on making sure she is.' Gil was

the one to answer and again his words had a distinct ring of authority that would put even the most sceptical person at ease.

Gil turned the oxygen on and Phemie put the tent—a crude frame of plastic pipes held together with tape and then covered with plastic wrap—over the baby. The oxygen slowly filled the tent, Gil monitoring the saturation levels and both of them watching the baby's response.

'What are you going to call her?' Phemie asked, glancing over at Gemma, who was lying back with her eyes shut.

'We're letting the children choose her name,' Ron announced when Gemma didn't say anything.

Phemie smiled and glanced at the wide stares of the children in question peeping around the doorframe. 'Fantastic. So,' she addressed the children, 'what names have you come up with for a girl? Was it a unanimous decision?'

'It was,' Selena, the third eldest, announced.

'And what shall she be named?' Phemie asked.

The children all looked at each other then back at the doctors, their eyes bright with delight. 'We're going to call her Rajene Paris.'

Phemie turned to look at the midwife, whose eyes were wide with unexpected delight.

'You name babe after me?' Her tone was filled with complete awe.

'You've looked after Mum and the baby so well,' Selena continued, standing proudly as she spoke. 'We all decided it was the best name ever—if it was a girl,' she added with a little smile.

'Well,' Gil announced to all and sundry, 'I'm happy to report that Rajene Paris's colour is improving, her skin is becoming less mottled and her little lungs aren't having to work so hard to suck in air.'

'Oh. Oh!' Gemma said happily, and then promptly burst into tears. 'Oh, my darling baby is all right.'

The children all clapped, and the little ones, the youngest of whom could only be about three years old, jumped around excitedly. Suddenly, he stopped and looked up at Yolanda, who had come back.

'Can I play now, Landa?' he asked.

'Yes, Lee. All of you can go play. I think Mum and Rajene Paris need some quiet,' Yolanda announced. Once the younger ones had run off, she looked at the adults. 'Peter's just radioed through to say the plane has landed. Melissa and Iris are on their way.'

'That'd be right.' Ron chortled. 'Now that the

drama's all over and every thing's as right as rain, they finally get here.'

Gil looked at Phemie and when he smiled she couldn't get over the way his gaze encompassed her. Together, they'd been able to care for mother and baby, which was their job. In that look, though, there was more. Gil's eyes radiated his happiness, his pride at what they'd done as a team.

Half an hour later, as they stood on the verandah looking at the land as dusk started to approach, Gil put his arm about her waist and drew her close. Phemie didn't stop him. She wanted to be held by him, to cap off this special day by being close to the man she was most certainly in love with. Seeing the way he'd cared for that baby, especially knowing how his own baby girl had been taken from him, her heart churned with love.

She loved him. She loved Gil and whilst she knew it was so incredibly wrong, that it could never be, she wanted this moment. Melissa and Iris were taking care of mother and baby, the Etherington children were helping to tidy up and make dinner and Rajene had been ordered to sit, relax and have a cup of tea. All seemed to be right with the world.

'We did it, Euphemia.'

'Yes, we did.' She snuggled back into him and sighed, covering his arms with her own. Gil dropped a kiss on the top of her head as they both simply stood and stared, absorbing the serenity. 'When I first heard the baby's cries, I thought everything was going to be fine. I thought, We've done it. And then she started...' Phemie stopped and shook her head slightly. 'And then I turned and you'd set up your makeshift oxygen tent. Genius, Gil. Pure genius.'

'I'm sure you would have come up with something even better. You're amazing at thinking outside the square box.'

She laughed without humour. 'I disagree. I don't see that in myself at all.'

Gil looked at her with a quizzical furrow on his brow. 'Well, then, I must disagree with your disagreement. On the train, for example, you were the one to get the RFDS organised.'

'I had a phone that would reach them.'

'And with Mary, in Sydney, you were the one who came up with the best way to move her.'

'Mary.' She sighed again, although this time it was one of remorse. She pulled Gil's arms around her, needing to feel more secure. He was more than happy to oblige and dropped a kiss on her cheek.

'You are not to blame for her death.' Gil's words were adamant.

'I know. I'm sorry about that night, Gil. I didn't mean to take my frustrations out on you.' Phemie angled her head so she could see him better and couldn't help smiling when he dropped a kiss on the tip of her nose.

'No need to apologise. You shared an amazing time with Mary and I'm positive you'll never forget her. You are quite a woman, Euphemia Grainger. You care. You give. You put yourself on the line for everyone else. Isn't it time you did something for yourself? Accepted your reward?' He turned her in his arms and without waiting pressed his mouth to hers. Phemie kissed him back with all the love in her heart, wanting him to know, to feel, just how much she appreciated him, how much she needed him, how much she wanted him.

'I want to know everything about you,' he murmured against her mouth, punctuating his words with kisses. 'I want to spend my precious time here, chatting to you in every spare moment we have. I want to hold you, to kiss you, to simply be with you.'

'Sleep with me?' she asked, and he didn't miss that hint of hesitation in her tone.

A small smile touched his lips and he raised both eyebrows. 'I am a red-blooded male, Euphemia.' His voice was deep and filled with repressed desire. 'However, given the time constraints and other…geographical factors, I don't think such a course of action would be advisable.'

Phemie couldn't believe that she actually felt hurt by his words. She knew he was being honourable, that he was trying to do the right thing, but by the same token was she yet again to be rejected? When Danny Ellingham had rejected her, she'd thought it was because of Anthony, because of the Down's syndrome, but perhaps all those years ago she'd been wrong. Perhaps he'd simply been rejecting *her* and she hadn't realised it. 'You don't find me attr—'

Gil stopped her words by pressing his mouth to hers, showing her rather than telling her just how incredibly attracted he was. 'How could you even think that? From almost the first moment I saw you, I've yearned to have you in my arms, your body pressed to mine, my mouth worshipping you.' He looked intently into her eyes. 'You have come to mean so much to me in such a short time. You're special, Phemie. Very special, and very dear to me.'

'Gil. Listen I—'

'No. Please.' He pressed a finger to her lips. 'I heard what you said before, about never marrying.'

'I can't.'

'Why not?' He tightened his arms around her but pulled back, the pleading note in his voice showing he really wanted to understand. 'What I feel for you...' He stopped and shook his head. 'I didn't ask for it. I most certainly didn't expect it but Phemie, I've been in love before and this...what I feel for you...' He stopped again, trying to be diplomatic in his choice of words.

'Don't, Gil.' Phemie twisted out of his grasp and walked to the other corner of the verandah. As the sky was now changing colour, indicating the sun was indeed setting, she began to realise how tired she really was. She didn't have the strength to argue with him so instead she allowed his words, his sultry deep voice to wash over her.

'Phemie. You must allow me to tell you how I feel. To tell you how these feelings we're both experiencing don't come along every day.' He turned her to face him and took her hands in his. 'This is rare. So fast. So illogical but there it is. *You* feel it. *I* feel it. We were destined to meet.'

'Destined?' Phemie laughed without humour

and pulled away from him again. 'No. There is no destiny, Gil. There is only shuffling around the cards we've been dealt, trying to find the best possible hand to play.'

'You've been hurt.' It was a statement. 'Did some man hurt you? Destroy your confidence? Break your heart? Is that why you came to the outback? To hide your light under a bushel?'

'No. You've got me all wrong, Gil. I wasn't hurt, or dumped or jilted. I came to the outback because I'm a coward.' She spread her arms wide. 'There. The unvarnished truth about the woman you think I am.'

'You are not a coward, Euphemia.'

'I am. I have been stuck in a rut my whole life. Doing what needed to be done and then being too scared to take a step into the unknown. Even Anthony had the guts to leave home long before I did. He's travelled and he's had adventures and I haven't done any of those things.' She hiccuped, unable to believe the level of emotion she was feeling saying these words out loud, especially to Gil.

'Anthony's "steps" into the world have all been orchestrated for him,' Gil replied calmly. 'Even his trip to Sydney was undertaken with the aid of a supervisor. Your parents would have prepared him for these eventualities so that—'

'But they never prepared me.' Phemie couldn't believe that tears were pressing firmly behind her eyes. She wiped them away with an angry hand. 'I love my parents, please don't misinterpret me, but for my whole life Anthony has been the main focus—for all three of us. He has *always* had to come first.' She looked down at her hands and was surprised to find them trembling. 'I love him, Gil. He's my brother but sometimes…sometimes I used to wish I was an only child, that I had that "normal" life the other girls at school had. I didn't want to be known as the girl with the Down's syndrome brother. That was my identity until I finished high school. I know none of this is Anthony's fault, or my parents'. They did the best with what they had but I didn't get to have an ordinary childhood and the scars of that still run very deep.'

'It's quite clear to all and sundry that you love him, Euphemia.' Gil came towards her again, holding out a pristine white handkerchief. 'But whilst you were growing up, you just wanted a bit of the attention. Correct?'

'Yes.'

'And then you felt guilty for wanting that?'

'Yes.' She nodded, unable to believe he understood. 'You have no idea what it felt like to grow up in that sort of…box. There was nowhere for me to go. No means of breaking out. My parameters were set.' She dabbed at her eyes and shook her head, giving him an ironic smile. 'And then, when I was in med school, my parents dropped another bombshell.'

'What?' Gil held his breath, completely unable to predict what she might say next.

'They told me I was a carrier. If I have children, there's a probability they'll have Down's syndrome.'

'Carrier?' Gil frowned. 'Down's is caused by a random event to the reproductive cells *before* conception.'

'Except if you're a carrier of a defective translocation trisomy 21 chromosome. Which I am and so is my mother. They had me tested when I was a teenager, although I had no idea what the tests were all about back then.'

And there it was. Gil almost sighed with relief as he realised that this was Phemie's road block. Now that he understood the problem, he could fix it. Fixing problems was what he did best and if he could help this most incredible woman, the woman who had helped him realise his heart didn't need to be locked away for the rest of his life, that it was strong enough to love again, then so be it.

'That is why you won't marry?'

'I will not subject my children to the life I've had. I know you can rationalise things and say that because I know all about Down's, that it's not as bad as other disabilities, I'll be better able to deal with it. I know I can point at Anthony and say look how well he's turned out. He's a stable and functioning member of society. He's independent and happy and now my parents are off having the holiday they never thought they'd have, but it was all still a very restrictive upbringing.'

'But you could overcome this, Phemie.' His words were clear, calm and very matter-of-fact. 'You would make the most wonderful mother and together—*together*—we would handle anything life threw at us, even if it was a child with Down's. You have your parents' experiences to guide you, plus your own experiences, and you would be such a perfect mother. I truly believe that, Phemie. There is no reason for you to be afraid. You are strong and powerful and incredibly independent.'

She heard what he'd said but still felt as though she had to make him understand where she was coming from. 'But you don't understand what my life was like. I ended up being so used to having my life ordered, structured down to the minutest detail, that when Anthony and my parents left, I had no idea who I was. I was a grown woman. I was a doctor. I worked at a hospital. I was good at caring for others but I was lousy at caring for myself.' Her breath caught on a hiccup. 'Do you have any idea what it feels like to look in the mirror and not recognise the person staring back at you?'

'Yes.' His reply was quiet and Phemie stopped her ranting to look at him more closely. 'Yes, I do, and it's terrifying.' He paused. 'When I received word of June's and Caitie's deaths, I shrank from the world. I *put* myself into the same sort of box you were raised in so, yes, I do understand. I understand the helplessness. I understand the isolation. I understand the way you rationalise things to keep yourself protected, safe.

'Then something happens and you're forced to take a step out of that boxed existence.'

'The fellowship?' she asked and he nodded.

'No doubt someone gave you the idea to come help in the outback.'

'It was Dex.'

'I should have guessed. He's a good guy and

doesn't like to see obvious talent going to waste.' Gil came closer but made no effort to touch her. 'We're more alike than you realise, Phemie. Even though we were both stuck in a rut, even though we were no doubt extremely lonely, confused and wondering just how to get out—the fact is that we both did. We sucked in a deep breath and took the plunge—and look at what's happened?'

'We found each other,' Phemie whispered, then shook her head. 'But I can't have children, Gil. I just won't do that.'

'Understandable.'

'What?'

'I understand what you're saying, why you're saying it.'

'And you agree?'

'If you feel that strongly about it, then yes.'

Phemie frowned. 'Just like that?'

'You've made the decision, an informed decision, and I'm positive you've no doubt done a lot of research into this matter...' At Phemie's slight nod, he continued. 'But you shouldn't be punished by spending the rest of your life alone. Loneliness isn't for someone as beautiful as you. It would eat you up inside and you don't want that.' He wanted to caress her cheek, to touch her, to reiterate his words with actions, but he stood his ground, keeping the distance between them. He needed, more than anything, for Phemie to be the one to reach out to him. He'd come so far and he'd wait, no doubt impatiently, for her to come the rest of the way. If this was going to work between them, it needed to be a two-way street.

'But don't you want to have children? You've been a father once and I saw the look in your eyes when you held the baby earlier. You want children, Gil. I can see it.'

'I do, but there is more than one way to become a parent.' He closed his eyes for a moment then looked at her with an intensity that made her knees start to quiver. 'Phemie, I'm almost certain I'm falling in love with you. I also have an inkling that you may feel the same way.'

'Yes.' Why wasn't he making any attempt to take her back into his arms? Was he about to tell her that even though he felt that way, even though she'd just admitted to feeling the same way, they still couldn't be together? She held her breath.

'That's…' His smile was deep, encompassing and she breathed easily. 'That's wonderful to know.' Still, he stayed where he was. 'However, I think we need time,' he continued. 'We need to sit and talk and get to know each other more. There is still so much I don't know about you.'

'And I about you.'

'See? Let's take this week. Let's use it to our best advantage.'

'And then?'

'And then I need to return to England.'

Phemie's heart caught in her throat at his words and her eyes widened in pain. The thought of not having him there, not having him with her, made her feel ill. 'But— No!' She stepped forward and wrapped her arms about his waist, burying her face in his chest, her ear pressed to his heart so she could listen to it beat its comforting, steady rhythm.

'Shh.' He enveloped her, relieved she'd come to him. 'I'm not going to stay there. I know you can't leave Australia and I would never ask you to. You have your family and your much-needed work. Simply being here, in the outback, even for just half a day, has already shown me the importance of the Royal Flying Doctor Service.'

'You were a part of that team today.'

'And it was enlightening, exhilarating and utterly exciting. I have not felt so…thrilled with medicine since my time in Tarparnii working with Pacific Medical Aid. There, the medicine was even more raw than it is here and sometimes much more devastating than the car crash in Sydney, but being there, helping others, spending time with those poor orphaned children, becoming integrated into the community—it was that which saved my life. When I returned to England, life didn't seem so bad but I still had no idea exactly where I was supposed to fit any more. Even with the fellowship, I knew I was just putting off the inevitable.'

'Which is?'

'Finding out who I am and where I fit in the world.'

'And do you know that now?' She was gazing into his eyes as she asked the question and Gil smiled brightly before brushing a kiss across her lips.

'I'm starting to.'

She smiled and breathed him in, loving his scent, loving the feel of his body beneath her hands, loving everything about him. 'Good. So we use this week?'

'Yes.'

'Then you go back to England.'

'Yes.'

'And then?'

'And then I apply for a permanent job here.'

'Just like that?'

'Why not?'

'Is it really that simple?'

'My life in England…it's not there any more. It's here. With you.' He kissed her again. 'Simple as that.'

CHAPTER TWELVE

FOR the next week, Phemie and Gil spent almost every moment together. They would eat breakfast, learning what each other preferred. Phemie was more than happy to eat cereal or toast but Gil preferred a cooked breakfast.

'Besides, it's cooler to cook in the mornings than the evenings,' he pointed out on his fourth day there.

They attended clinics, house calls and two emergencies. Each time Phemie watched Gil closely as they flew in the small aircraft but he either hid his loathing for flying very well or he was coming to terms with it, letting go of his past.

In the evenings, if they weren't called out, they'd take it in turns to cook and then either watch a movie or play cards or, Phemie's favourite thing, sit on the porch swing and look at the stars, talking softly and intimately.

When it was time for bed, Gil would kiss her softly, tell her that he loved her and then head to

his own room. He insisted it was the right thing to
do and Phemie realised that chivalry wasn't dead.
As the end of his week drew closer, their time
together became more intense.

'I don't want you to go,' she said at breakfast as
she watched him finish cooking his bacon and
eggs. She poured them both a cup of rich-bodied
Australian tea, which just so happened to be Gil's
new favourite drink.

'I don't want to go. I want to stay here with you,
work with you, spend as much time with you as
I can. However, I do need to tie up quite a few
loose ends.'

'You'll call me after each leg of your journey?'

'I'll do my best. Just make sure you're somewhere that has good reception.'

Both of them were putting on a brave front for
a goodbye they knew was going to be extremely
difficult. 'We'll email and call,' he murmured,
pulling her to his side. He switched off the frying
pan, not feeling particularly hungry. Today he
would make the trek from the base to Perth, then
Adelaide and finally to Sydney. There, he'd meet
up with William and the rest of his staff before
they all flew back to England the next morning.
'I'll be back here before you know it.'

'Just as well you have such impressive credentials or else the RFDS might not have wanted to
employ you. Ben even told me the word "over
qualified" was bandied around,' she teased,
needing to do anything to lighten the atmosphere.

'Just as well,' he replied, and caught her to him
for a long, luxurious kiss. 'I love you, Phemie. I
want to be with you. Always.'

'I know.' She also knew he wasn't looking
forward to this flight. Tomorrow, especially, was
almost a twenty-four-hour flight from Sydney to
Heathrow. Gil's family had been taken from him
before and she knew he was concerned that this
time everything should go according to plan.
'Everything will be fine.' They both had to believe
that, to keep focused.

Nothing more had been said about children but
the fact that Gil accepted her reasons for not
wanting to have her own had made Phemie relax.
That he hadn't pushed her on the subject also
meant he had a plan up his sleeve, that much she'd
learned about him during this week. He was so incredibly smart and he would ponder and think
things through quite thoroughly before voicing
his thoughts. She would therefore trust him and in
doing so she found she was finally able to let go

of the enormous weight she'd been carrying around for far too long. Gil had helped her realise that her parents had done the best job they could to give her a good childhood. It may not have been the 'cookie-cutter' family home she'd thought a lot of other girls lived in but it had been solid. It couldn't have been at all easy for them yet they'd done what they'd had to do and Phemie knew she was very much loved by them. Wasn't that all that really mattered?

When the time came for Sardi to fly Gil to Kalgoorlie so he could make the connecting flight to Perth, Phemie found her throat completely choked with emotion. Both of them were waiting until the last possible moment before he boarded the plane.

'I love you,' she whispered against his mouth as she kissed him, tears streaming down her face.

'Don't cry, love.' He held her tight, gripping his second chance at love, not wanting to ever let her go. He so desperately wanted her to go with him, to visit England, but he knew she couldn't leave, not at the moment. Her work here was precious and necessary and he respected that. Soon they would be running the base together. He'd have more time to write articles and he had a new scope of inspiration before him—adaptive emergency medicine. He would start by writing up how to make a humidicrib from nothing more than Gaffer tape, plastic pipes and kitchen sandwich wrap.

'I can't wait to get back,' he murmured, his eyes bright with love. 'I'd say keep the home fires burning but I think you'd best keep the fans whirring instead,' he joked, and was rewarded with a little laugh. With one last, heart-searing kiss, he boarded the plane, Madge pulling up the stairs behind him. All the RFDS staff had been welcoming and this past week had been one of the happiest he'd had in a very long time.

As the plane rose, Gil looked out the window at his beautiful Euphemia, standing next to the airstrip, waving. He watched until she disappeared from view.

'But *when* will the plane be here?'

Anthony's impatience was even worse than her own. Phemie walked into the front office and asked Ben to radio Sardi to check.

'I radioed her three minutes ago.' Ben was a rational man but he could quite understand Phemie's need to know everything about this flight. 'But I'll radio again.'

'Thank you, Benjamin.' She patted his shoulder and headed outside to where Anthony was peering up at the sky. She picked up his hat from the verandah and placed it on his head. 'Don't forget your hat, darling. The sun is super-hot here.'

'Yes, Phemie,' he responded, and she couldn't help but hug him close.

'I love you.' She was so proud of everything he'd achieved. He was her baby brother and, as such, was so vitally important to her. It wasn't too late, she realised, to achieve that sibling relationship with him. All she needed to do was to let go of the picture perfect family image she'd had in her head and move forward to what she had. Anthony was a great brother who loved her. What more could a sister ask?

'I love you, too, Phemie,' he replied in his normal voice, eyes still glued to the sky. 'I'm going to be the first one to find the plane. I'm good at that, and heaps of other stuff too.'

She laughed and danced around him, her excitement unable to be contained. 'I know you are.'

'I'm good at finding planes.'

'You're the best, and this plane is *my* kind of plane.' Gil was coming home. Home to her. To where he belonged. The past month had been the longest of her life but they'd spent the time talking and finding out more about each other.

Gil had turned down job offers, sold his apartment, made arrangements for his 'jalopy' to be transported to Australia and packed his belongings. The last time he'd moved had been when his family had died. Now he was moving *towards* his new family and he couldn't wait.

Gil's impatience was mounting. 'How much longer, Sardi?'

'Three minutes since you last asked me,' Sardi returned, but smiled, understanding his need.

Gil had been flying for, what felt like for ever, which he guessed it was, given that he'd simply been either in a plane or in an airport for the past couple of days, not wanting to stop over and spend the night anywhere, instead preferring to get to his Euphemia as soon as possible.

Finally, they were there, the hangar and the house getting larger and larger as they approached.

He looked out the window and saw Anthony jumping around excitedly, waving his arms about. What surprised him more was to see Phemie joining in with the jumping and the waving. He laughed, pleased she was excited he was back.

They'd talked so much on the phone and whilst

he knew the separation had been good for both of them, giving them time to think things through, to be one hundred per cent sure this was what they both wanted, he had never been so glad to return to a place as he was right now.

'Wait until I land the plane first,' Sardi called jovially as Gil impatiently drummed his fingers. He'd been in this plane enough times to know how to operate the doors. The instant the wheels touched the runway, he unclipped his seat belt and checked his jeans pocket, patting the ring concealed there. Everything was ready.

Gil didn't know who was more impatient, himself or Euphemia, but the instant the plane door was open, she was in his arms, his mouth on hers, and they were reunited in a fire of passion and need.

'I love you,' she murmured against his mouth as she kissed him, tears of joy streaming down her face.

'Why are you crying, Phemie?' Anthony wanted to know.

'Because I'm happy,' she called over her shoulder, her arms still tight around Gil, never wanting to let him go. 'I'm so very happy.'

'I'll bet I can make you happier,' Gil said softly in her ear, and in the next instant, right there in the middle of the airstrip with the plane's engines still whirring behind them, he eased away and dropped down to one knee.

'Gil?' Phemie's eyes were wide as she looked at him.

'I didn't want to do this over the phone. I needed to be here, with you. To see your face, to watch your eyes light with amazement. Euphemia Grainger, you have no idea just what you do to me and I want you to keep doing it for the rest of my life.' He held her hand and to her utter astonishment he slipped on a diamond ring. 'Will you marry me?'

She gasped and covered her mouth with her free hand, a fresh bout of tears starting up. 'Oh. Oh.' This was it. She hadn't realised it until the moment was upon her but this was definitely it. Standing there, hearing Gil's words, safe in the love she could see reflected in his eyes, Phemie knew there was nothing more important in her life than achieving her own happiness, and Gil was the one who had not only helped her to realise it but was the one who was providing it.

All those years ago, when she'd cried herself to sleep, her mother stroking her hair, telling her that one day she would meet a man who'd love everything about her—well, that day was today and Gil was most definitely that man. Happy? She was more than happy. She was blissfully content, wrapped in his love and secure in the knowledge that whatever their life threw at them, whatever might or might not happen with regard to children, they would face their future as one.

'Oh, Gil,' she whispered again.

'What's the matter, Phemie?' Anthony wanted to know. 'More happy tears?'

'Yes. Oh, yes.'

'Was that answer to me or Anthony?' Gil asked.

'To you,' she said softly. 'You come first.'

Gil stood and swooped her up into his arms, spinning her round a few times as he kissed her.

'*We* come first,' he corrected. 'You and me. Together.'

'For ever.'

EPILOGUE

'WHEN will the fireworks and stuff start, Phemie?' Anthony asked.

'Soon. Very soon,' she told her impatient brother. 'You keep watching the sky.' They were all gathered in the main street of Didja for the annual New Year's Eve fireworks and Phemie knew she'd never had a happier start to the coming year.

Last year, she'd preferred to stay at the RFDS Base, seeing the New Year in by going to bed early and waking up the next morning with a headache. This year, she thought as she hugged her husband close, would be so very different.

In a few weeks time, both she and Gil would head over to Tarparnii for three months to work with Pacific Medical Aid. The RFDS would send another doctor to the Base to cover them until their return…and when they returned their numbers would increase.

Gil had indeed had a plan brewing and when

he'd talked about the amount of orphaned children in Tarparnii and the poor sanitation most villages experienced, Phemie's heart had turned over with need. The more he'd talked, the more Phemie had wanted to see these places for herself, to see those children and help in any way she could.

'When will the adoption be final?' Iris asked Phemie as they all stood together, waiting for the fireworks to start. Iris held her squirming daughter, Anya, in her arms and when the toddler saw Dex, she squealed with delight. Iris put her down and watched as the little girl ran over to her adoptive father.

'One month after we arrive in Tarparnii.'

'That's fantastic. Instant motherhood isn't easy,' Iris laughed. 'I should know having inherited Anya upon her parents' death but it's…' she sighed with happiness. 'Fantastic. You and Gil are going to love being parents.'

Phemie smiled up at her handsome husband who was busy talking to Joss and a very pregnant Melissa. 'I think we will.' She had a sparkle in her eyes and a glow which was perfectly radiant. She had some special news to share with her husband, news she was sure he wouldn't quite believe but she wanted to wait for the right moment. 'We have so much love to give, to share with our children.'

'Love does that,' Iris confirmed.

'When will the fireworks and stuff start, Phemie?' Anthony asked again and Phemie checked her watch.

'It's almost midnight, Anthony. One more minute.' Excitement coursed through Phemie as Gil tightened his arm about her waist.

'He's so excited,' he murmured, brushing a kiss to Phemie's lips. 'It's addictive.'

Gil had loved his first outback Christmas and now seemed to be intent on enjoying his first outback New Year. Phemie's parents and Anthony had been resplendent at their September wedding and had been more than happy to return to Didja to share in the newly weds' first Christmas. A few days later, the Graingers had left for another short holiday, Anthony wanting to stay on to experience New Year in Didja and who could blame him? The atmosphere was indeed electrifying.

'You're addictive,' Phemie returned and urged his head down for a more thorough kiss.

'Hey,' Melissa protested. 'You're supposed to wait until midnight actually strikes before the kissing starts.'

'You can talk,' Dex teased his big sister as he

tickled Anya's tummy. 'Last year, you and Joss almost couldn't wait to lip-lock.'

Joss grinned at Melissa. 'Our first kiss and now—a year later—look where we all are.' He placed a hand protectively on his wife's belly, caressing the baby within.

'It's been quite a year,' Gil agreed, smiling at his Euphemia. He'd never thought he'd ever be this happy again and yet every day, his love grew for the woman at his side. He loved outback life, loved the vast, remoteness of it all and couldn't wait to fill their home with the children they both yearned for. Soon. It would all be happening soon.

'When will the fireworks and stuff start, Phemie?' Anthony asked and Phemie giggled as the ten second countdown began. Soon, she would tell her husband the good news, the most amazing news. When Melissa had confirmed Phemie's own suspicions, she hadn't believed it.

'Would you like me to do an amniocentesis to check for Down's?' Melissa had asked and Phemie had declined the offer. Gil had been right all those months ago. Together, with him by her side, she could do anything. She would make the most wonderful mother and he would be the most incredible father.

'Keep watching the sky,' she told her brother. 'It will light up your life.' She, however, wasn't watching the sky. Instead, she was looking as intently into Gil's eyes as he was into her own.

'You light up my life,' she murmured.

'Ditto,' he replied and kissed her passionately as the fireworks cracked and sparkled above them.

'By the way,' she murmured against his lips with utter happiness filling her heart. 'I'm pregnant and I've never been happier in my life.'